THE DWIMFOLK

JAMES BROGDEN

THE DWIMFOLK

ISBN
978-1-80394-559-0
978-1-80394-558-3 (signed edition)

2 4 6 8 10 9 7 5 3 1

Design & Layout by Michael Smith
Printed and bound in England by Short Run Press

ABSINTHE BOOKS
PS Publishing | Grosvenor House
1 New Road Hornsea, HU18 1PG | United Kingdom

editor@pspublishing.co.uk | www.pspublishing.co.uk

Represented by:
Authorised Rep Compliance Ltd.
Ground Floor, 71 Lower Baggot Street
Dublin, D02 P593, Ireland
www.arccompliance.com

Introduction

James Brogden is the author of novels such as *Hekla's Children, The Hollow Tree, Bone Harvest, The Plague Stones* and *The Strandling*. His first novel was *The Narrows*. UK-born, he spent part of his childhood in Tasmania before returning to live in the West Midlands. His novels frequently feature aspects of folklore, as evidenced by the titles above—and *The Dwimfolk* is no exception.

The story follows Wren, a young boy who lives with his mother in a village that struggles to accept either of them. The pair keep themselves to themselves, their behaviour weird in the locals' eyes, and are seen as outsiders because of that. Wren lives a part-feral life, wandering through the fields and woods, especially a place called The Trod—and within that, the Deep Trod.

Lisa, a supply teacher new to the village, tries to assist Wren, to bring him into the school environment and help him integrate with the other children. The events that follow her arrival—and interaction with Wren—couldn't have been foreseen by anyone in the school, or even the village. As she fights to make sense of what's happening, she discovers that the truth of Wren's life is stranger by far than she'd imagined.

And now she's part of it.

To say any more would be to reveal too much, and *The Dwimfolk* is a delight. So read on, and let yourself travel the Deep Trod with Wren.

—Marie O'Regan
Derbyshire,
April 2025

THE DWIMFOLK

For Jeremy

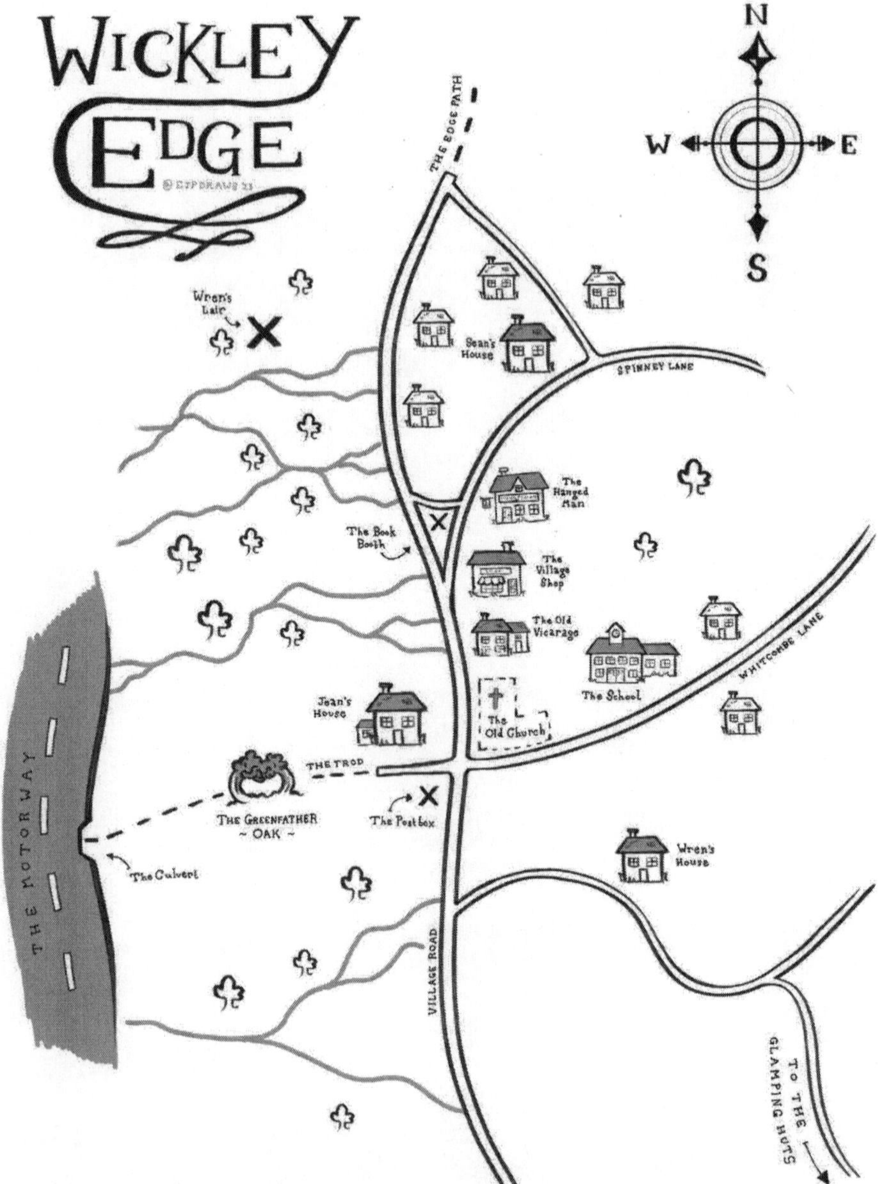
WICKLEY EDGE
N
W
E
S
THE EDGE PATH
Wren's Lair
Sean's House
SPINNEY LANE
The Hanged Man
The Book Booth
The Village Shop
The Old Vicarage
The School
WHITCOMBE LANE
Jean's House
The Old Church
THE TROD
THE MOTORWAY
The Greenfather ~ OAK ~
The Postbox
The Culvert
Wren's House
VILLAGE ROAD
TO THE GLAMPING HUTS

Story Time

Lisa Bradshaw couldn't be sure exactly when the hollow-eyed boy had entered her classroom. It was only after she'd gathered her pupils together on the big rug at the end of the day—all sitting neatly and cross-legged, with their faces solemnly attentive for the next chapter of their home-time story—that she did a quick head check in case someone was hiding in the toilets or eating the crayons, and saw him.

He was at the back, hunched behind Jessica Hollin and Faizal Baig, peering between their shoulders. His face was as pale as milk, and his eyes glittered beneath an unkempt fringe.

"Hello," she said, pitching her voice low and gentle. "You must be Wren. I was told I might expect you. Would you like to stay for the story?"

He moved so quickly it seemed he was halfway out of the window before she'd closed her mouth. He was running across the playground as she stood and by the time her class were all shouting, he'd cleared the fence and disappeared into the woods on the other side.

Heart pounding, Lisa watched the green shadows into which he'd melted, but saw no movement. He didn't reappear. It was easy to imagine that he'd never been there at all, except that her class had all run to the window and were shrieking.

"Miss, where did he go?"

"Miss! Miss! He jumped out of the window!"

"Miss! I think he touched me!"

"Miss! He knocked over the brushes!"

"Miss! He *jumped* out of the *window*!"

She calmed and cajoled them back onto the mat, which didn't take long as there were only eight of them. St Luke's was a small village Middle School serving a wide rural area and, by necessity, the ages that would have been kept in separate classes in a larger school had to be combined, the result being that her class of "Saplings" included children who had just turned nine and those who were almost eleven—a huge age gap at this stage of their lives. After Edward Trevis had used his inhaler and Olivia Wormald had been to the toilet, they were all sitting as before—but wide-eyed and jittery as if an electric current was running through the room. Lisa took a sip of water and replaced the glass beside her chair.

"Now then," she said. "Who can—"

Every single hand shot into the air.

"Jess."

Jess Hollin was the oldest, and Class Captain, trusted with the solemn responsibilities of putting out the pencil pots at the start of the day and wiping the whiteboard at the end. She had a sensible ponytail and her mother packed a lunch in small, artfully arranged portions in a bento box, and Jess ate every bit.

"You scared him, Miss," Jess said.

"Scared him?"

"Yes Miss. He doesn't like to be seen. You're not supposed to see him. If you do, you have to pretend that you didn't, otherwise he gets scared and runs away."

"I want him to run away!" said Faizal. "He smells!"

There was giggling, and Lisa shushed it. "So." She surveyed the solemn faces. "You've all seen him before."

Nodding. Edward was waving his arm like he was trying to land a plane.

"Edward?"

"Only, at the end of the day, Miss, he likes story-time. Usually when it's Mr Blake he stays outside and listens through the window, but you've got a quieter voice, so I think he wanted to hear better."

"Is Mr Blake going to get better?" asked Olivia

"We all very much hope he will," Lisa replied, feeling that this conversation was in danger of becoming derailed. Maybe she should have just gone back to the adventures of Charlie Bucket.

"My mummy says that we have to pray extra special hard for him," said Polly Duncombe.

"Who?" asked Edward. "Mr Blake or Gollum?"

Lisa blinked from one of them to the other. "Gollum?"

"That's what everybody calls him, Miss," said Jess. "Nobody calls him Wren."

"I bet his mum does," said Faizal.

"His mum's a witch anyway," added Edward. "They say he eats cats and baby birds." He was grinning ghoulishly.

"Now I'm sure that's not—"

"*I don't want him to eat Pumpkin!*" wailed Olivia, and they were off.

It took longer to calm them again, and she was able to read only a few pages before it was home-time and the bell rang. After the tumbling chaos of bags and coats and tidying away, Lisa went across the corridor to ask Jean about the boy.

Jean Allsop was the headmistress and teacher of Oaks, the combined class of Year 7 and 8 children, the oldest of whom would be going on to upper school in town at the end of the year. She was also the bursar, registrar, nurse, and she washed the PE kits of the poorest children in her own home. Lisa found her stacking the chairs of her own classroom, and lent a hand.

"It sounds like your lot had a fun time," said Jean. "You want to watch that. There's a danger that the little darlings will actually enjoy themselves."

"Sorry, I hope they weren't too noisy."

Jean waved it away and stacked another chair. "I wouldn't worry. Noise is just a child's way of being loud and annoying."

Lisa laughed. "That's . . . profound, I think?"

"It's nothing of the sort. It's facetious and unprofessional, forty years of winging it distilled right there." She arched an eyebrow at Lisa over her spectacles. "But then if you can't be facetious and unprofessional every now and then, what's the point?"

"The thing is," said Lisa, "the children weren't exactly enjoying themselves. We had a visitor."

"Ah," Jean replied. "Finally showed himself, did he?"

"Just like you warned me he might. When you told me at the interview that one of the local boys was school-phobic and might pop in from time to time I sort of thought he might come in with his mother or father and be wearing a uniform, not suddenly appear out of nowhere looking like the ghost of Peter Pan. They call him Gollum, apparently."

"I know. Children can be cruel. I expected he might have shown himself sooner, but he was probably not sure about you, new teacher and all. Poor mite's probably confused and frightened."

"Well that makes two of us."

"Oh, Wren's never hurt anyone. He's eccentric, yes, but basically harmless. He just wants to hear a story now and then. The fact that he came in at all is good—he could have listened from outside the window, but you've got him interested. That's a start!"

"A start," she agreed, wondering what it was that she'd started. "I suppose it couldn't hurt for me to put out an extra chair for him," she said.

◆ ◆ ◆

Lisa made her goodbyes, collected her marking, and went out to her car.

It was mid-September, and despite having done the journey to Wickley for the past fortnight, she still liked having her phone's satnav to guide her to the motorway, as the village was surrounded by a labyrinth of narrow lanes between high hedges and copses of woodland. This time it told her that there was an incident on Village Road between Wickley and Stanton; the road on the screen was coloured a deep red, and the estimated delay was over forty minutes. No idea what that was about. Probably two tractors having the Staffordshire version of a Mexican standoff.

Instead, the satnav was suggesting an alternative route—down Bumble Hole Lane. The holloway. The Trod. She hadn't thought that it was a through road, but according to the screen it looked like it arrowed straight across country for a mile from Wickley Edge before going underneath the motorway and into the town, where she could pick up her junction and shave ten minutes off her normal travel time.

Nevertheless, something about it gave her the creeps. She'd never walked down it—only explored as far as the post-box on the corner almost buried in a holly hedge. Past the lips but not over the teeth, so to speak. It looked like it became quite dark and narrow, and she was surprised that the satnav was suggesting it, but supposed there were lots of hidden shortcuts like this, known only to the locals and not ordinarily suggested by the app's algorithms.

She looked at the screen again. Angry red line versus clever shortcut. *Oh yeah,* she'd say offhandedly tomorrow to Jean, *I just took the Trod, you know.*

"I bet it's the local dogging spot," she muttered, and started the engine.

It was straight across at the post-box, and if it really was called Bumble Hole Lane there was no sign. She saw immediately that it was a single lane with no room for two normal-sized vehicles to pass, let alone anything like a tractor, and she didn't relish the idea of having to face down an irate farmer or reverse all the way back. The best she could hope for was that there were some passing spaces.

The lane sloped downwards, becoming narrower and darker. The holly hedges on either side rose higher the further she went, until she was driving between earthen banks through which the roots twisted like cables, and the hollies had become replaced by thicker, older trees that reached their limbs overhead, curving to meet in an unbroken canopy so that she needed her headlights, which was ridiculous at half past four in the afternoon, and gave the impression that she was driving through a murmurous, undersea gloom. The tarmac degenerated into ruts and potholes before giving way to a dirt track muffled by the accumulated leaf mould of uncounted autumns. Lisa could no longer fool herself that this was a navigable right of way. The only upside was that she was less likely to encounter something coming the other way, which was just as well, because so far she'd seen no passing places.

The dot on the screen that was her still appeared to be back at the junction with Village Road, and when she looked closer, she saw without surprise that there was no phone signal. She had no idea how far she'd driven. It felt like she should be coming out of the woods into open fields, but by her dashboard clock it had been barely five minutes. She was going to have to turn around, but the holloway was too narrow for a three- or even three-hundred-point turn. She wasn't even sure there was enough space to open her door fully.

Still the track sloped inexorably down.

She tried not to imagine what would happen if it just kept going down and never rose again, becoming darker and narrower until she couldn't see anything and the sides of the holloway pressed so tightly on either side that she couldn't open the doors at all. Not to imagine being trapped and screaming, watched only by the indifferent trees, but maybe not only them, maybe something else, long-limbed and hollow-eyed, its skin as pale as milk.

Something bumped against the roof. Bumped, slithered and scraped. *Branches*, she told herself. *Just some low-hanging branches, that's all*. But she couldn't recall having seen any in front of her just now.

"Oh this is *bollocks*!" she shouted.

That was when she nearly ran over the old man.

He was pressed up against the steep bank on the driver's side, shouting.

She yanked the wheel to the left, but there was no left for the car to go to, and felt a shudder accompanied by a squealing of tortured plastic as her front bumper fetched up against the holloway's bank. The car stalled. She sat gripping the steering wheel, breathing hard, her mouth full of the sour aftertaste of adrenalin.

"You can't bloody drive down here!" he yelled at her through the window. "It's a no-through road!" He wore brown corduroy trousers tucked into wellington boots, a waxed jacket over a checked shirt, and a look of furious incredulity.

She unpeeled her hand from the wheel and pushed the little button that locked the doors, then unscrolled the window, but only an inch.

"I'm so sorry," she replied. "Are you all right? I had no idea—my satnav directed me this way."

"Bloody satnavs! Ounce of common sense'd do you tourists more good than a bloody satnav!"

In her head she shot back *Well if it's a no bloody through road then maybe somebody with an ounce of bloody common sense should have put up a bloody sign, shouldn't they?* but what she actually heard coming out of her mouth were more muttered and feeble apologies. It didn't look like she'd hit him, thank God. He'd sprung half up the bank to get out of her way, like a wiry old mountain goat. He looked like he was about to expand on his opinions about tourists, presumably with his ideas about young women drivers, before his expression abruptly softened.

"Wait up," he said. "You're the new teacher, aren't you?"

He'd recognised her. Great. "What if I am?"

"Well look now, I'm sorry if I came on a bit strong just then. I thought you were some idiot trying to find a shortcut. We get them, you know. It's just that the Trod's a public right of way and there's folks using it all the time. There'll be kids walking back from school in town and the near-misses we've had along here, well, it doesn't bear thinking about. Oh!" He stuck his hand out. "Tim Fredericks. I'm at the Old Rectory. Pleased to meet you."

She stared at his hand, her own mental satnav struggling to make sense of the unpredictable bends and curves of this conversation. Then she reached through the window and shook it. "Lisa," she said. "Bradshaw."

"Ah, like the guidebook." He nodded as if this made sense. "Hell of a shame about Simon, isn't it?"

"Yes, well I'm sure the doctors are giving him the best care they can." And then, before he could take advantage of the opportunity to hold forth about the state of the NHS, the state of his own health, or, God forbid, try to engage her in small talk, she added quickly, "I'd actually be very grateful if you could please let me know if there's somewhere up ahead I can turn around. I don't much fancy backing up that."

"You should be all right," said Fredericks, scratching his head and looking back the way he'd come. "The Trod pretty much bottoms out here. She'll start to rise again—not so high as the village, but you'll soon be out in fields. Turn around in the first gate you come to, but don't try to carry on—you'll never get under the motorway. And most importantly," he added, with a grin and a wink which she was sure he thought reassuring, "don't trust the bloody satnav!"

She gave him a pursed-lip smile and touched two fingers to her forehead in a little salute, and pressed on. In her rear-view mirror he watched her for a moment and then turned to resume his journey up the Trod.

Fredericks' advice was sound, though. A little further on the lane levelled out and began to rise, widening as it did, and soon she was driving between perfectly ordinary hedgerows—still high and close on either side, but without the peculiar sense of brooding watchfulness that fell with the shadows from the overarching trees. Half a mile ahead was the wooded embankment of the motorway and the dark slot through which Bumble Hole Lane ran, and no, there was no way any vehicle bigger than a quad bike could get through that. Why the fuck had her satnav presented it as a driveable route? Then there was a break on the right where a gate let into the field; she couldn't open it, but at least it gave her enough space to get out and examine the damage. It wasn't much—just a bit of scratched paintwork. She was able to execute a clumsy turn, even though she had to back right into the hedge on the other side to do so. Its branches clutched and scratched at her car's paintwork with a squealing like nails down a blackboard and eventually let her go, but begrudgingly, it seemed, as if to say *Fair enough, you made a mistake so we'll let you go this time. But don't try this again, new teacher, or next time we'll hold you here for the things in the Trod.*

Mercifully, she didn't encounter anybody else on her way back, and was thankful not to meet any kids walking home from the big school in town. The embarrassment of having one of her class come to her tomorrow and say that someone's big sister or brother had seen her driving along the holloway would be unbearable. She didn't even see Fredericks, which wasn't surprising; he had the look of a man who could put on a nice turn of speed in full rambling mode, but couldn't stop herself from imagining him being scooped up by roots and dragged into the bushes.

She expelled a huge sigh of relief when she finally saw the post-box again, and turned right onto Village Road. She sat for a moment, gathering herself. If anything pulled up behind her they could just sodding well wait.

The bright blue line of her satnav route had realigned itself in its familiar direction. It still said there would be a delay, but at least it wasn't trying to lure her down a road that didn't exist. Getting home late would be a small price to pay—smaller certainly than whatever was waiting for her in the Trod.

Trying to dismiss the experience as nothing more than fatigue, anxiety and an overactive imagination, she shifted into gear and set off.

This is How I Meet the New Teacher

I FLEE SCHOOL FOR THE SAFETY OF THE WOODS AND hide in the trunk of an old ash tree. The Deadalive Ash, I call it. You'd think it was dead if you only saw the big black cavern of its inside, but its branches are lush and it must be hundreds of years old. I feel its protective shade around me, and slowly I calm.

Who is she? What's happened to Mr Blake? I mean yes, that was the first time I've been to story-time since the start of term and yes, my best mate Sean is in the next class up so it wouldn't affect him, but still, you'd think someone might have told me. How do we know this new teacher is any good? Her voice is too soft. Mr Blake has a lovely deep Welsh voice which surrounds you like a blanket and the little'uns curl up on the mat and have a nap while he's reading, but hers is high and scratchy, and she didn't do any voices.

When my panic has subsided to a dull resentment, I stash the crayons I stole in the Deadalive Ash and creep back to the school as Squirrel. I hide under the staff-room window and listen to them talk about me—how she thinks I shouldn't be allowed to just roam around wherever I like, as if I'd ever hurt any of the little'uns; how she thinks I should be in normal school. Just like what the woman from the council thought, before Mama and I put a stop to her questions.

From the trees above the road, I watch the new teacher get into her car and leave, and I follow as she stupidly tries to drive down the Trod. Where does she think she's going? I race ahead, jumping from branch to branch. It's not hard to beat her because she's driving very slowly. Suddenly I'm furious. I don't mean just angry—I mean proper seething. How dare she replace Mr Blake? How dare she be here? Who does she think she is, driving down here like it's any old road?

I'll show her what it's really like.

I run ahead to the Greenfather Oak, press my lips to the bark and whisper, and the Deep Trod opens.

She almost goes in.

I don't know what goes wrong. Maybe because she's in a car, with all that metal and plastic, or maybe because my birthday's tomorrow and the Trod's saving its energy for me. It's not an exact science. She skims the edge, and through the windscreen I watch her expression change as she realises that she's not where she thought she was, but then she slips out of it like a trout that won't be tickled. Then Mr Fredericks is there so I scarper.

Everything is all higgledy-piggledy and I feel out of sorts.

Checking on my skulls will make me feel better.

My Secret Lair is Like This

The woods covering Wickley Edge are surprisingly thick; they've grown wild along the ridge for ages because it's too steep and rocky for farming, and even though they're quite narrow—only about a hundred metres either side of the ridgeline—when you're in them, they feel like they go on forever, because you can't see anything of the outside world.

The west-facing slope is steeper and rockier, etched with hidden gullies that you can fall into if you don't know where you're going. A short way along and off to the left there's a hole in the ground, which is impossible to see because of the camouflaged screen I've placed over it. I discovered it ages ago by falling in and nearly breaking my neck. Now there's a knotted rope tied to the trunk of a hardy old holly. I sniff the air as Hare but there's nobody nearby so I remove the screen and climb down, dragging the screen back behind me. It's a drop of only a few feet but the hole is narrow and stinks of soot and grease because it used to be a chimney.

People discovered ages ago that sandstone is easy to dig out, especially if erosion has already made some natural caves, and it didn't take somebody much effort to widen and deepen this one, squaring the entrance for a door, carving holes for windows, and boring a chimney up through to the surface. Nobody except me knows it's here because at some point after it was abandoned there was a landslide and the whole front got buried, and it was forgotten. What's left is, I think, the kitchen, the larder and a bedroom. The chimney comes down into a wide fireplace in what used to be the kitchen.

There's a candle in a saucer by the hearth, which I light. I could see perfectly well in the dark as literally anything other than Boy, but then I wouldn't have the use of my hands and besides, I like the flickering. On one of the walls, I'm drawing a big map of Wickley Edge to mark out the borders of my realm, which is what I need the crayons for. There's also my stash of emergency supplies: tools, clothes, food and, of course, my books. All in case I need to get away from Mama for a bit. I suppose there might be another landslip one day, but hopefully I'll be with the Greenfather by then and I won't need my skulls.

I have a shrew, a squirrel, a fox, a hare, and a little pyramid of birds that I can't identify, but it doesn't really matter because there's only one reason to go as Bird and they all do that. What I'd really like is a deer—there are muntjac in Wickley Woods but so far I haven't found one. The smaller animals were fine when I was little, but these days Shrew just feels demeaning, like having to wear baby clothes. I could probably work out how to trap and kill a deer, but I've got no idea what to do with the rest of it, and that would just be a waste. I'm not a monster.

My skulls are arranged in a circle around a big candle in the middle of the kitchen floor. I take a gorse thorn, prick the tip of my forefinger, and paint a smear of blood on each of them to strengthen their connections to me.

I feel a bit calmer after this.

It's quite easy to clean an animal skull. You boil off all the soft bits and then, when it's cooled, you soak it in some bleachy water. Mama doesn't mind, so long as I don't use any of her good saucepans. She seems to think it's educational—at least it keeps me occupied—and I don't think she cares what I do with them afterwards. I can't talk to her about the new teacher because I'm not supposed to go anywhere near the school, so Kevin will have to do instead. I check my twigger materials and make a mental note of what needs replacing: clematis bark, ash keys, blackthorn spikes. Yes, I have enough bits to make Kevin again.

What a Twigger Is and How to Make One

A TWIGGER IS A TEMPORARY BODY FOR ONE OF THE Greenfather's courtiers from the Deep Trod. The different ways you make them attract members of different courts, because they all have their preferences—some like bone, others favour bark, a clockwise binding for one, a pinning with blackthorns for another. Kevin is the one I usually make—my go-to option when I'm bored or need cheering up. He's got a forked beech twig for a torso and legs, arms attached with criss-cross lashing of red and blue string, padded with bell heather. His head is a walnut shell, which is over-sized and makes him a bit top-heavy and prone to falling over, but preferable to hazelnut, which just seems to attract troublemakers for some reason. Usually when I build a new twigger I have to take it to the Greenfather Oak for quickening, because it's the closest place to the Deep Trod, but I've made this walnut-headed idiot so many times that the connection is strong enough for him to quicken wherever I make him.

Other than Sean, Kevin is the closest thing I've got to a friend.

The moment when a bunch of dead forest matter quickens with the life of a courtier is a shivering and trembling, like the gasp when you surface from underwater or the first in-drawn breath of a newborn before the scream begins, and I always watch it closely because I suspect that Kevin isn't really as dumb as he appears, and in this first moment I think I should be able to get a clue about what he really is, but so far I've been unsuccessful.

Kevin totters upright, all ten centimetres of him. "My prince," he says solemnly. The creases in the walnut shell do for eyes and a nose, and the split between the two halves of the shell is a reasonable mouth. He bows, overbalances, and falls flat on his face. He does this every time.

"Morning, Kevin. How goes the Court of the Leaf?"

"Eternal in its verdant splendour under the wise and beneficent rule of thy green father, my prince," he replies.

"Hmm, the less said about him the better."

He cocks his little head to one side in a pantomime of concern, since he can't do facial expressions. "Art nervous about thy birthday on the morrow?"

"I don't want to talk about that yet. Tell me about the new schoolteacher."

He shrugs. "Alas, I am but a simple factotum. I fetch, I carry, I know no more."

"If you say so." I tap his head and he falls over again, turning it into an elaborate court-jester tumble and somersault, and comes up laughing.

"Ta-daa!" He knocks on his own walnut-skull, cups his hands and calls "Hello?" then mimics his own echo: "Hello-ello-lo-o!" He shrugs again. "Nothing there. The candles are lit, but the castle is empty."

Yes, Kevin's an idiot, and I suspect he may be lying to me, but he does cheer me up.

"I've thought of a new name, by the way, my prince," he says.

"Oh really?" I know he dislikes Kevin as a name, and would prefer something more jesterly like Hubbub or Master Nonesuch, but I enjoy winding him up.

"Henceforth, I shall be known as..." he announces, striking an impressive pose, "Timothy Claypole!"

I pretend to consider this. "No, still not good enough. Kevin it is."

He deflates. "Very well, my Prince."

"If you can't help me, I'm going to have to make someone who can. Fetch me that robin's egg."

It takes most of the afternoon to build what I need. A twigger is only ever good for one use, since some courtiers can be very powerful, and the strength of oak and bone and stone can quickly get used up trying to house one of them, so the twigger might only last a few moments before falling apart. Sometimes it will take days to make one tough enough to last for a meaningful conversation. This one doesn't need much because it only has to answer three questions.

When the twigger is finished it looks like a stick man made out of actual sticks. It's bound with clematis bark and for a head it's got a bright blue robin's egg that I collected back in spring because I like to be prepared and you never know when this kind of stuff might come in handy. Robins' eggs are useful for all sorts of things—summoning the Court of the Air, obviously, because it's a bird. There were two in the nest, but I left the other to hatch because I'm not a monster. This one must have been close to hatching because if I shake it gently I can hear tiny bones rattling inside like grit. I have to be super-careful making a hole for the twigger's mouth without breaking the whole thing, and I carefully wad it into the head framework with moss and feathers. By this time Kevin has disintegrated, but it's okay, I'll make him again later.

By the way, one thing that you never do is use an actual animal skull for a twigger's head. The Inner Court—the Court of Bone—is not something you want to mess with unless you really have to.

After I made my first ever twigger—a clumsy little tripod of a thing that trundled around making small squeaking noises for a few seconds until it fell apart—I asked Mama, "Who showed you how to do this?" I must have been five years old. She smiled and cuddled me (this was back in the days when she still did that) and said, "You did, my little Wren!" I didn't understand. "When you were a tiny baby in my tummy, too small to even make a bump, I started to know things: about the trees and the animals and the things that come from deeper in the Trod. And as you grew into a bigger bump, I came to know more things, and I knew that it was the wisdom of the Greenfather reaching into me through you, so that when you were born, I could teach it all to you and you could be ready to meet him." That made perfect sense to me. As I say, I was five. It didn't occur to me until years afterwards to wonder exactly how I got into her tummy.

I take my new twigger to the Greenfather Oak at the bottom of the Trod. It's actually two big oak trees growing on either side of the holloway. They're ancient, hundreds of years old, maybe even over a thousand, and their roots have spread out and grown together so that you can't tell where one stops and the other begins—not only that, but two of their big lower branches have also grown so close together that they've merged, like they've melted together. *Inosculated*, the word is. I looked it up. It comes from the Latin word for kissing. Sometimes it actually does look like they're in love, but other times it looks like they're strangling each other. The Greenfather Oak is the gateway to the Deep Trod, and if you approach it the wrong way you might slip through. I can feel the Deep Trod pressing on the other side of the air like the heaviness before a thunderstorm, and I place my new twigger gently among the roots in the middle of the path, tucking it right down.

Then I climb out of the holloway, find a tree trunk to sit against, and wait.

I don't mean to fall asleep, but it's been a busy day so far.

I'm awoken by the sound of heavy footsteps thumping along the Trod.

I don't have any way of telling the time other than the sun, but I know it must be around teatime now. Someone is using the holloway as a shortcut to come from town. I creep from my seat as Fox, first on all fours, then on my belly so that I can peer over the bank to see who it is.

It's my arch enemy, Aidan Preston.

He's slouching along, school bag over one shoulder; probably been hanging around with his mates doing whatever it is they do. He's got earbuds in, and I relax. He can't hear me. I could pop a balloon right behind him and he wouldn't hear me. Then my sense of security evaporates as I realise that the twigger is still down where I left it to quicken and he's walking straight towards it with those clumping great shoes.

I come about as close as I ever have to panic. If he crushes that twigger it'll be months before I can make another one like it. I find myself standing as Boy again on the bank's edge, breathing hard, fists clenched by my side, and a rock in each one. I wonder where those came from. It doesn't matter—Aidan is half a dozen steps from where I hid the twigger and I try to calculate from his pace whether he's likely to step over it or on it, and I know that if he does step on it I'm going to fling these rocks at his head. They might only be sandstone, but they're hard enough to do some damage.

And I am a very good shot.

Three paces.

Two.

I raise the rock in my right hand.

He steps over the twigger's quickening place without seeing it and slouches on his way.

I drop the rocks, almost disappointed.

When I'm sure that he's safely distant and there's nobody else coming, I skid down the bank and retrieve the twigger. It is alive in my hands. I can't be sure exactly what is wearing it, only that it's likely to be of the Court of Air, which on the one hand is good because they see a lot of what happens on the ground, but on the other hand they're not the easiest to hold a conversation with. This thing is all twitters and chirrups, and the bones in its shell-skull are rattling with either excitement or agitation.

The binding is already unravelling, and I know that I don't have much time to question it, so I find the nearest bush to hide in.

I ask the first question: *where is my father*?

I always ask this, not that I'm expecting a helpful answer, and its response is the usual mystical rubbish. He could be worlds away, or he could be just behind your shoulder. The Greenfather comes and goes as he wishes, and cares not for boys so arrogant as to claim his blood blah blah blah. More binding frays and one of its legs falls off. It chirps in dismay.

I ask my second question: *is Sean still my friend*?

The twigger scoffs at such a childish request, doing its best to sound like its dignity has been offended. Did I really bring it out of the Deep Trod for such trivialities? But the answer isn't trivial to me, so I press it and the twigger answers: *Sean Curran remains your most steadfast of allies*.

So that's all right then.

The twigger by now is little more than a loosely woven jumble of splinters and bark fibres, but I hope I've got the chance for one last question.

I ask it: *can the new teacher be trusted*?

No, the twigger responds immediately, then utters an ear-piercing little shriek of laughter and disintegrates completely. The robin's egg implodes and the tiny bones of its long-dead chick fall through my fingers like breadcrumbs. I brush the remains from my palms and think about this for a long time.

My Birthday Goes Like This

NEXT MORNING, I HOLD THE HOLLY MASK UP TO my face while Mama ties the cords at the back of my head. Her fingers are quick and sure, almost impatient, and when she tugs on the free ends the prickly leaves are pulled close against my chin, cheeks, nose and forehead. I can't help but wince.

"Stop wriggling," she scolds. "Wriggling is for worms."

"Sorry, Mama," I say, trying not to move my lips too much. I should be used to it by now. I offered to make the mask myself, because then I could have avoided the worst of the thorns getting in my eyes, but she insisted on doing it, which is probably just as well since it's one less thing she can blame me for when it goes wrong again. Part of me feels resigned to the inevitable disappointment, but I can't deny the little shiver of excitement that comes with each prickle and scratch.

It is my birthday, after all.

I've told Sean and the other kids in the village that I'm going to be twelve. It might be true. It's as good a number as any—the months of the year, the signs of the zodiac, the number of toes on a three-legged fox that's had to gnaw its foot off to escape a trap. Kidding. If you add the one and the two together you get three, which will be the size of our family when the Greenfather finally comes for me.

Mama won't tell me how old I am, if she even knows. She'll get confused sometimes and spend ages thinking it's one year when I can just go into the village and look at the newspapers in the shop and find out, or maybe she does it deliberately to mess with my sense of time. She says that as the Greenfather's son, age isn't important, but I'm a lot bigger than I was this time last year and the impatience in her hands says that maybe we haven't got many birthdays left.

"There," she says, and turns me around to face her. "That will do it. He'll see you and know you for his own this time."

Mama's mask is lime-washed terracotta, so that the Court of the Earth will accept her, and it hovers in front of me in the darkness like a pale full moon. Behind it, her eyes rove over me, looking for any flaws that might cause the Greenfather to reject me again, and I raise my head and pull my shoulders back, trying to look proud for her, even though her scrutiny makes me feel more uncomfortable than I can remember. I don't know why it should. I'm naked, just like before. The forest shapes that she painted on my skin are no different. All the same, I want to shrink from her inspection, but I won't. Wriggling is for worms.

Other than her mask she's naked, too, also painted with forest shapes but nothing special, just the ordinary ones you'd use for protection in a place like this. The Greenfather might not be around, but there are members of Courts other than Leaf and Earth who don't know it's my birthday and wouldn't care anyway, even if they understood the concept, which they probably don't. Her dreadlocks are untied and hanging free behind and in front, which is good, because I don't want to look at her breasts, and I am grateful that it's not quite dawn yet, so that I can't see any more. Sean said that Aidan Preston showed him pictures of naked women on his phone once, and we looked for some on Sean's because I don't have a phone, but I couldn't work out what those women were doing—all I know is that the thought of Mama without clothes makes my stomach feel like it's full of eels.

We are standing at the deepest point of the Trod. Even if it were daylight we wouldn't be seen, because the trees grow so thick—oak and ash and holly and hawthorn and elder—that they screen it completely from the outside world. In the daylight they form an arched roof of shifting green high overhead. Direct sunlight almost never reaches here, and everything drifts in a kind of underwater dimness.

There's little chance of anyone coming along the Trod this early. Even if they did, there's nothing they could say that hasn't been said to us a thousand times before—or sneered in the street, or shouted from passing cars, or daubed in dogshit on our front door, or scrawled on notes wrapped around rocks thrown through our windows.

Freaks.

Perverts.

Devil worshippers.

But that's okay. Mama takes care of me and I take care of Mama.

"What are you waiting for?" she whispers. "Tell him you're here. Tell him to come for his son. You know the words."

I do. I've said them every year since I could talk. She mistakes hesitation for fear, but I stopped being afraid on my tenth birthday, when I realised he wasn't coming for me then, and never would. I don't know what's going to happen when I'm a teenager—the ones I see in town are slouching, hooting creatures with their faces jammed in their phones or onto each other's mouths—but I've already decided this is the last time I'm going to say the words. I suppose like any last thing I want to hold on to it for just a bit longer.

I draw a deep breath and begin.

"Hear me, Greenfather. I am Wren, son of Cassandra, whom you lay with upon a time." I never knew what that meant until just recently, but now I think about Sean's phone and those eels squirm a bit more. "I have lived in the sun for twelve years and today is my birthday, and I ask you to claim me for the green, that I might know my father."

The silence of the trees and the shadows of the Trod fill the hole left by my voice.

When I was little, she said it for me until she thought maybe that was why he didn't come and so she made me do it. The first time, when I was six, I got it wrong, which was why he didn't come then, and I got a hiding. For my seventh she made me repeat it over and over—with a hiding for each slip or stumble—and I said it perfectly, but he didn't come then, either. She said it must have been because he didn't recognise my voice, so for my eighth she made the first of the masks.

Mama is stretched forward, listening. I start to speak but she slaps me quiet.

"He hears you," she whispers. "Say it again."

"Mama, I don't think—"

"*Say it again!*"

So I say it again. And again. Over and over, just like every other time. And I think maybe the deeper blackness where the phantom shapes of tree trunks are swallowed lengthens, possibly, like something stretching, or reaching. My arms go all goose-pimply and my ears catch something just out of range. If I could go as Bat I'd be able to hear it properly, or as Fox I'd be able to see whatever's down there, but the other thing about the mask is that the holly thorns make me stay as Boy, which is how Mama says I should present myself.

"He hears you!" she gasps, and claps her hands in delight. It's rare that I see her happy, never mind like this. Childlike. "He's coming to take you home! Go to him!" And she gives me a push, so I do what I'm told. But it's like one of those dreams; I know that I'm putting one foot in front of the other, I can feel roots pressing into the arches of my feet and the leaf mulch squeezing all cool and slimy between my toes, but I can't tell if I'm making any progress.

This is the Deep Trod. The place of my father, and of the Courts of the Dwimfolk.

"Call to him!" she orders. There's desperation edging her voice now. "Tell him who you are!"

I say the words again but it doesn't make any difference. That weird sense of stretching-reaching dwindles, and the holloway is just its normal self again—the Deep Trod has withdrawn itself from around us. The trees are just trees, the high banks to either side are just earth and roots and bracken, and when Mama takes her mask off her face is stricken. The Greenfather hasn't come. I've done it wrong again.

I could easily run off as Hare and escape the hiding that's bound to follow, but what would be the point? I'd have to go home eventually. So I take a deep breath and head back towards her.

"Mama," I say. "I'm sorry. I don't know what I—"

Her hand, lightning-quick, cuffs me on the left ear.

"You think this is a game?" she spits. "You think you can just parrot the words and that's enough? You think he can't tell when what comes out of *here*—" she flicks my jaw "—doesn't come out of *here* as well?" She jabs my chest with a forefinger.

There's no point replying. I shouldn't have tried to apologise. Best let her get on with it. I tune out her yelling and slapping and instead sniff the air as Fox in case anybody is nearby who might overhear. Past her sweat-and-patchouli-and-lager smell there's the loam and leaf-rot underfoot, the green sappiness of the undergrowth—nettles, meadowsweet, and a patch of wild garlic not far off—the dryness of the sandstone like old cake. In the fields up past the woods there's sheep-shit and a hint of diesel, but it's at least a day old, we're too early even for farmers to be up and about, and nobody is on the holloway for half a mile in either direction.

It's possible that Mama mistakes my sniffing for tears—if so, it seems to satisfy her, because she leaves off the hiding and starts getting dressed. Carefully I reach behind my head and untie the mask, then I put my pants and shorts and t-shirt back on. She reaches into her bag—it's huge and made of a dozen different colours of wool knotted together and I've never seen inside it—pulls out a ten-pound note and hands it to me.

"Here," she says. "Go into town and do whatever *normal* boys do on their birthday."

I watch her trudge away back up the Trod towards the village.

I'm less upset about this than I thought I'd be—much less upset than Mama—because I know that basically nothing has changed. I'm still a prince of the Green and in my father's absence I have a realm to protect. It's barely dawn, and nothing will be open for hours yet, but I've got plenty of things to keep me busy in the meantime.

The Borders of My Realm

WHERE THE TROD RISES AGAIN, THE WALLS BECOME shallower and widen out, the trees thin, and soon it's fields on either side and you can hear the motorway. I don't know which one it is. The M6? I don't really care. It's not like I'm ever going to travel on it. One good thing about the Deep Trod is it's the one place where you can't hear the motorway. It sounds like the ocean, not that I've ever been to the seaside, but I've seen it in videos so I think I've got a fair idea.

Another half-mile along what is now a farm track with thick brambly hedgerows either side, and you can see it. The motorway embankment is a high green wall, a rampart, like you see on old hill forts. There's a screen of trees along the top—mostly hawthorns hanging with tattered plastic—but you can see the traffic swishing by on the other side.

Cutting through the embankment is a culvert to take the track under the motorway, and that's where my power ends. Obviously I can go through it as Boy, just not as anything else, which is ironic because town is the place I wish I could go as something that can escape easily—Squirrel, say, or Rat. Mama tries to make sure we get as many of our supplies as possible from Wickley, but there are some things, like her medicine, that can only be got from town and she won't set foot in the place, so I have to.

Stanton is full of eyes. People stare at you in the street and in the shops, and they stare harder if you're a boy who doesn't look like he fits in. Their eyes are hard and so are their voices, and so are their fists if they catch you. The inside of the culvert is full of their graffiti and cigarette ends and other horrible things that I don't know how they work and don't want to, but it doesn't spill out into the Trod because it's where *their* territory ends, too.

The only time I ever convinced Sean to bunk off school with me was to throw stones at the motorway. It's not as bad as it sounds. We hid in the trees behind the crash barrier and just lobbed them blindly in the general direction, so it's not like we were actually *aiming* for anyone, and they were *really* small stones, just bits of gravel, to be honest, but we could definitely hear the *tink!* whenever one of us scored a hit. Sean was beating me five points to three when Mr Fredericks came walking along the path on his way into town and shouted what the effing eff did we think we were doing, so we legged it. I don't know if he recognised us, or if he said anything, or whether just being seen was enough to give Sean the willies, because he didn't speak to me for two weeks.

I'll try to catch him before school this morning and see if he wants to come into town with me afterwards; we can probably buy enough sweets with ten pounds to make ourselves sick.

As Bird, I leave the Trod and fly above Wickley Edge. It's dawn now, and I start at the motorway culvert, catching thermals that rise off the concrete and soaring high to watch the shiny beetle-crawl of cars, then I dive and skim back along the holloway, flitting just above ground level, plunging into the cool, deep green. At the top of the holloway, where Bumble Hole Lane crosses the Village Road by the weird overgrown plot where the church used to be, I flit left and past a small triangular village green which is just large enough for a red telephone box and a park bench. On the other side of it is the Hanged Man pub and Wickley Village Hall. If I flit to the right I'll go past the vicarage and the school, but I'm not interested in those yet. Further on it's houses, and one of them is where Sean lives.

It's a biggish old house, because he's got two younger sisters and one younger brother and his parents Chris and Debbie own a wholefood shop in town. Because Sean is the oldest he's got his own room, and I perch on his windowsill. The window is open because we've been having some hot and sticky weather, even for September, and he's lying asleep face-down on the covers in just his pants. Sometimes I wish I had a bedroom like Sean's, with posters and shelves with books and Lego on the floor and a wardrobe piled with boxes of old toys and drawers to put clothes and a football and a cricket bat. But then if I did, where would I put my skulls?

I climb in as Boy and, because I don't want to wake him straight away, I go over to his washstand where I check my face in the mirror. The scratches from the mask aren't as bad as I'd thought. I clean them, trying to be quiet, but he wakes up anyway.

"Wren?" he murmurs. "What are you doing in my room?"

One of the reasons why Sean and I are best friends is because he's one of the few people who can pronounce my name properly. The silent W is tricky.

"It's my birthday."

"I know," he replies. "Happy birthday. I was going to give you a card. But it's..." He looks at the time on his bedside clock, groans, and buries his face in the pillow.

"Mama gave me ten pounds," I explain. "Come with me into town after school and we'll spend it."

"Okay," he says, his voice muffled. "Can I go back to sleep now?"

"Can I play on your phone?"

He just grunts and turns his head to the other side which I take to mean yes.

Sean's parents bought him the phone for his birthday—his is in March, which makes him older than me by six months, but he doesn't make a big thing out of it. It's a pay-as-you-go and he has to earn the money to top it up by doing chores. He told me that his dad said it was to teach him the value of hard work and to never take things for granted, which makes sense if you can't sneak into anyone's house as Shrew or Squirrel and help yourself to their things whenever you like.

I'm not interested in any of the social apps because I know what everyone in Wickley thinks of me, or the games where you pretend to run around killing things, because if I wanted to do that I'd just go out into the woods and do it. The games I like are the ones where you have to match tumbling coloured blocks or unknot pieces of string or make water flow through pipes. I can get lost in them and lose track of time and forget where or who I am, because they don't mean anything. I'm good at them, too. I can solve puzzles quicker than anyone.

I do this for a while and then get bored, so I start flicking through his photos while he snores. As I say, I'm not interested in gossip because all the other children at St Luke's are idiots, but one photo stops me. I sit looking at it for a long time.

It's nothing special, I tell myself. Just a group selfie, taken with four of the boys in his Leavers class, their grinning heads crowded into the frame against a blue sky. Impossible to see what they've been doing, but it's a fair bet they've been playing football. It's not like he's got his arm around one of them in particular. I don't even know their names. But all of a sudden, I know that when this school year finishes and next September comes around, Sean will be off to the big school in Stanton with these four and I won't be going with them. For a moment I'm tempted to delete the picture. He probably doesn't even remember taking it.

I look at him, lying asleep and drooling into his pillow. The early morning sunlight through the half-open curtain lies in a bar across his head. He's got very curly blond hair and in this light it looks like golden pencil shavings. He has a pink line over his right eyebrow which is a scar he got from when we were playing swordfights once. I got a bit carried away. He told his parents that he'd been running and had smacked into a tree, which is pretty much what happened if you think about it.

It occurs to me that I need to go to big school, too—not the actual kind of school where Sean's going, but when he leaves I can't still be farting around playing stick swordfights and going as little things like birds and mice. I think about the games on his phone; I'm going to need to Level Up.

I mean a human skull would be ideal but I've got to be realistic—short of lurking around the motorway and waiting for a fatal accident I'm not going to get one. I need to approach this systematically.

Domestic animals are easier to catch but likely to be missed, and that's a risk not worth taking. Being a bit odd gets you funny looks—being suspected of interfering with people's pets gets you a visit from the police or, worse, a social worker. Don't get me wrong, a dog would be great, but around these parts strays get shot by farmers. Livestock are obviously out of the question because who the fuck wants to be a cow or a sheep? Excuse my language.

So, something wild and big and a bit clever.

A badger, for example.

My head is spinning. Excited by the possibilities, I toss Sean's phone aside and lunge for the window, but I have enough presence of mind to climb out as Boy. He is my best friend, but I don't know what he'd do if he saw me as anything else.

Once safely outside, I rush back towards my lair through the woods, compiling a mental list of what I'm going to need: shovel, sack, wire-cutters, and a big knife.

How Me and Sean Met

When I was about five, a woman from the council came around to find out what Mama was doing about my schooling. I was too young to understand, but I've pieced it together since. Mama said that she was home-schooling me, and it's true, she was. Mostly in the ways of the Trod, to be fair, but also to read and count, and I was just getting the knack of writing. Her lessons were haphazard, and I think mostly to make me suitable for the Greenfather rather than to actually benefit me. Also, she doesn't like to leave the house if she can avoid it, and I was useless for running errands to the shops if I couldn't read lists or labels.

The visit from the social worker woman must have worried Mama because she decided it was time for us to make friends with other home-edders, at least for a little while; go to their meetings, join their outings, and keep the authorities happy.

Sean's family were already members. He goes to St Luke's now, of course, and I don't know how much of what happened that day with the twigger influenced their decision to give him a more normal childhood. At the time, though, he was like the rest of us, more a creature of the woods than the village. The group had a patch of woodland on the eastern side of the Edge where it's less steep and flattens out into the open countryside, and they'd dug a fire pit surrounded by tree-stump seats and a big tarpaulin tied to the trees. They had a shed with a turf roof where the grown-ups could sit and drink tea and gossip while us kids messed about in the woods. The older kids built shelters that leaked like sieves but served their purpose as places to snog, while us little ones made spears and bows and arrows and ran around like goblins trying to impale ourselves and each other. It's not clear what we were learning, but it didn't involve being in a school and that seemed enough for our parents. There was a lot of emphasis on crafting. We made pictures out of leaves and wove baskets out of grass.

Before our first visit, Mama ordered me to say nothing about the Deep Trod and I promised that of course I wouldn't, but it seemed strange—these kids were doing almost exactly the same things as me, how could they not know about the Greenfather or his courts or how to travel as an animal or make twiggers? And if they didn't know, how could they fail to be interested? But Mama insisted.

To be fair, she played her part—she didn't dump me and leave but stayed and made what must have been excruciating small talk with the other mums and dads, well aware of the village gossip and what they must have been saying behind her back afterwards. It was a relief to everyone when we stopped going after six months. The social worker lady must have been placated. Like I say, I was five and oblivious to all this. I didn't know it was a lie; I just thought I was making new friends.

Sean's younger sisters and brother were too young to roam freely, so when I first saw him he was mooching around an old hollow ash tree on his own.

"Don't get too close," I said. "The Court of the Earth will get you."

"The what of the what?" he asked, looking around.

"Nothing," I said quickly, realising that I'd broken my promise to Mama almost immediately. "What's your name?" I asked, to cover it up.

"Sean," he said. "What's yours?"

"Wren."

"Wren?" he echoed, saying it properly. "Like the bird?"

"Yes!" I was delighted. It must have been the first time someone hadn't said something like *That's a funny name.*

When you're five it doesn't take much more than that to become instant best friends, does it?

Sean and I were inseparable at home-ed club from then on. We climbed trees to neck-breaking heights, ate berries that probably should have killed us, and armed ourselves with long sticks to poke down rabbit holes unsuccessfully. I think if anything small and fluffy had come out we'd have pissed ourselves in terror and run.

Most of all, I spent a lot of time practising how to make twiggers.

I don't know if there's a proper name for them; Mama wouldn't tell me. She said I was too young, but I used to secretly watch her making them because just that spring I'd found my first skull and could spy on her as Mouse. I wasn't too young for *that*. Anyway, Aidan Preston—he of the dodgy lady videos—had a younger sister called Susan about my age who liked to light fires. Not big ones—she wasn't a pyromaniac or anything—she just liked to light a little fire in a circle of stones, sit and watch it and feed it leaves and twigs like a pet. I don't know what made Susan think it was a good idea to steal my twigger when my back was turned and feed it to her fire. She couldn't have known that it was anything other than a random jumble of sticks. It didn't matter. Whatever was in it was very unhappy about being on fire. The flames flared up, spitting sparks, much too tall for a fire of that size, and there were shapes in them. I didn't look too closely. I tried to tell Susan not to either, but it was useless; she was staring with her mouth wide open and a line of dribble hanging off her bottom lip. Suddenly she shrieked, collapsed, and started convulsing.

Then her big brother Aidan was there—not as big as he is now, of course, but still three years older than me which made him virtually a different species—and yelled, "You leave my sister alone!" even though I hadn't done anything to her, and he punched me in the face and split my lip.

The grown-ups came running—too late, of course. They dragged Aidan off me and dragged Susan away from the fire and calmed her down, but they couldn't get her to tell what had happened. They couldn't get her to tell them anything, and I don't think she's uttered a word since. Aidan has had plenty to say to me.

Mama knew that I had something to do with it, and our time with the home-edders ended shortly afterwards. Sean's parents pulled him out, too, and sent him to St Luke's, but we stayed friends.

Why I Don't Go Into Town If I Can Help It

THERE'S A PATCH OF EMPTY GROUND BETWEEN THE school and the Old Rectory, where the church used to be, overgrown and full of fly-tipped rubbish, and this is where I find Sean kicking a football around with two of the boys from that photo. One's got really curly hair and freckles and the other is tall with big floppy hands, like his body is growing faster than he can learn what to do with it. I hide in the trees and listen to their conversation in case they're talking about me. I've spent the day getting together everything I'm going to need and I'm in a good mood, but can't afford to get careless.

"…and then when you get to level twelve there's…"

"…not supposed to be giving us homework over the weekend…"

"…two weeks in a caravan with them, I'll go mental…"

But it's nothing I have any interest in, so I ambush them instead.

"Banzai!" I scream, falling out of the tree on top of them.

Flapper and Freckles recoil. Their faces are delicious with fright and Flapper actually loses balance and falls on his bum. Only Sean is grinning as he runs to retrieve his ball.

"Fucking hell, Gollum, you twat!" shouts Freckles. "What do you think you're doing?"

"Yeah, Gollum, you twat," says Flapper with stunning originality, wiping grass and mud off his arse.

Sean's face clouds. "Hey, don't call him that," he says.

"Yeah," I say. "Don't call me that."

"Then stop fucking acting like it!" says Freckles. "Sneaking around, jumping out at people, scaring the shit out of them!"

Flapper is getting to his feet and I watch, fascinated. It's like seeing a step-ladder assemble itself.

"It was just a joke," I point out.

"Well it wasn't funny!"

Bored of this now, I ignore them and turn to Sean. "Are you coming into town like we said?"

"What's he talking about?" says Freckles.

Sean looks confused. "Did we?"

My heart sinks, but it hardens a bit as it goes down. "Yes, we did. It's my birthday, remember?"

Freckles laughs, a high-pitched snigger. "Oh it's your birthday, is it Precious? What did you get for a present—a gold ring?"

I look at him. I think: *I've boiled the rotting flesh off a fox's skull and I can make its teeth my own. I bet you wouldn't be sniggering if you saw them coming at you one night when you're on your own, somewhere dark and lonely*. Maybe something of this reaches him, because his laughter dies and he looks away.

"Come on," he mutters, followed by something like *fucking loser* as he disappears with Flapper in tow, but it's really quiet.

"We agreed," I say to Sean.

"Wren, I was half-asleep. You woke me up."

"*We agreed.*" I can't help the pathetic wheedling tone of my voice, and it sickens me. Wriggling is for worms.

Sean, ever easy-going, shrugs and says: "All right, then. We also agreed that you're paying for everything."

"Yes, Precious!" I grin and run ahead.

◆ ◆ ◆

There's a sweetshop at the bottom of Stanton High Street called "World Candy." It sells the usual stuff plus a load of American sweets which taste funny—I don't know why, maybe they use different kinds of sugar. The shop is always full of kids straight after school, so it takes a while to get served, but eventually me and Sean load up and head for the playground.

The sign on the gate says that it's only for children up to the age of fourteen, so we go in and sit on the swings. All the same, Sean is big for his age and I look weird, and we start getting side-eye from the mums and dads of the little'uns even though we're just chatting. I try to be charitable and think they're being protective, but a lot of them are spending most of their time on their phones or gossiping with each other rather than playing with their kids, and I wonder how many of them would notice if one of their little darlings mysteriously disappeared. Anyway, Sean and I leave before we get told off.

All the bigger kids are hanging around the skateboard area, so we can't go there. Too old for one Court, too young for the other. There's a big duckpond bordered by weeping willows where we amuse ourselves by grabbing hold of the trailing branches and bungee-bouncing from them until we get told off by some miserable old fart, so we go to the bushes over the far side, where legend has it junkies hang out, to look for old needles, which I'm sure he thinks is much better.

"So who's the new teacher?" I ask.

"Miss Bradshaw? She's nice. Millie likes her."

"What's happened to Mr Blake?"

"He's ill."

"Ill? Ill with what? Is it serious?"

"I don't know, do I? Why are you getting so upset about it?"

"Because nobody told me! That's why!"

Sean gives me a funny look, and I realise that I've been shouting. "Why should it matter to you anyway?" he asks. "It's not your class. It's not like you even go to school."

"It doesn't mean I don't care."

"That's not what I meant."

"Well what did you mean, then?"

Sean stops, sighs, and rubs his hands down his face. He looks at me. "Do you want to have an argument on your birthday?" he asks. "Or do you want to hang out like normal?"

Yes, I want an argument. I want someone to yell and scream and kick and punch at, to get this out of me. I want him to know how angry I am that this is probably the last time we'll *hang out like normal*, but I'm afraid that if I do he'll leave and I won't even have that.

"Aren't you scared?" I ask him.

"Of what?"

"Of starting Big School."

He shrugs. "A bit. Not much I can do about it, is there?"

"You could run away and join the army."

He laughs. "I'm thirteen! I can't even legally get a paper round, you pillock!"

"You could lie about your age."

"What am I going to say? I'm a dwarf?"

"That'd be cool. You'd get a battle axe."

He smirks. "Don't need one."

"Why's that?"

"I've already got a massive chopper."

This is what passes for deep and meaningful conversation between boys our age. We laugh like drains and everything is all right again.

At least until Aidan Preston turns up.

We've found a big stick each and we're whacking the bushes as we amble along the path, not paying attention to where we're going, and I say to Sean: "So why didn't you go with Flapper and Freckles earlier?"

"Who?"

I explain.

"Oh, Mike and Craig?" He shrugs, like the answer is the most obvious thing in the world. "You got dibs. And you're my mate."

"But why?"

"Why what?"

"Why am I your mate? I'm weird, everyone thinks so. And they're good at football and things like that." I think, *you'll be going to Big School with them and I'll still be here and if I were in your position I'd ditch me now*, and that makes me feel like the world's worst friend. But he just says: "Wren, it's not like there's a checklist or something."

Could it be really that simple?

Maybe it could.

Maybe I could...

"Hey, look at the pair of batty boys!" laughs an older voice, cold and mocking. A crow's voice. Others join in, a murder of them. It's Aidan and his Year Ten mates, leaning in a line against the high rail of one of the skate park's half-pipes, peering over it at us. Flapper and Freckles are on the periphery of this court, hoping to be accepted, allying themselves with the dominant male. You can't blame them.

We've strayed too near their territory. This could be bad.

"Hey gay boys!" Aidan jeers. "Where are you off to?"

"Off into the woods to suck each other's dicks," suggests one of his mates and they laugh again—crowlike, apelike, doglike. I don't know who any of them are and genuinely can't tell one from the other. People are less distinguishable than animals, a lot of the time.

"Come on," mutters Sean, red-faced with impotent fury, and stomps off. I follow. I don't try to retaliate—not even to glare at them as Fox like I did with Mike and Craig, who in comparison now seem to be my oldest, bestest chums. There are too many of them. Even if it were just Aidan on his own, he could still kick the shit out of us.

Aidan wolf-whistles as we go. "Why don't you do us all a favour and fucking hang yourself like your dad, you fucking freak?" he caws. He's not going to come after us. We're not that important—just opportunistic targets for whatever it is swilling around inside him. I'd be insulted if I weren't so relieved. I wonder, where does it come from—all that muscle and anger?

Sean glances at me anxiously. "Don't listen to them," he says. "They're twats."

But it's all right. The man who lived with Mama before I was born wasn't my real father, so it doesn't bother me in the slightest. I wonder if I should appear to get upset because it's what they're expecting, but in the end I can't be bothered with whether or not this lot think I'm normal since they're basically animals themselves. No, it's not me I'm worried about, it's Sean. What's going to happen to him when he goes up to Big School and I'm not around to protect him?

We hurry out of the park.

Sean's mum and dad own the whole food shop in town. It's called *Nature's Intention* and it's got dozens of big Perspex hopper dispensers full of oats, raisins, flour, spices, pasta, milk powder, lentils, you name it, and it smells warm, all curry and nutmeg and cloves. Other than the stuff in the dispensers, they sell things that are mostly made out of bamboo or recycled plastic, and sometimes when I think about maybe staying in the mortal world and growing up, I think I could make those kinds of things—wooden toothbrushes and soap-holders and such. I'd be good at it, but it would still be a last resort.

Sean's dad Chris likes me. He's got lots of curly hair and glasses and a beard and whenever I stop by the shop he gives me a piece of his terrible flapjack from the counter. I think he's worried that I don't eat enough.

"All right Mowgli?" he says with a grin and hands me a slab of something which, from the state of it, is a new recipe: cranberries and sawdust.

"Hi Chris." He's the only one that calls me Mowgli. It might be insulting from anybody else, but I get it.

Sean's mum Debbie always seems a bit cold. She's nice enough but she doesn't like a joke the way Chris does. I think she thinks I might be dangerous for Sean, and I wonder how much of that is down to what happened at Forest School.

I hang out for a bit and help restock some of the hoppers and when they're about to close up for the day I make my goodbyes and go off to teach Aidan Preston not to fuck around with a Prince of the Green.

If You're Going to Fling Shit, Make it Fox

I WAIT UNTIL IT'S GETTING DARK.

When I find Aidan and his mates they've moved on from the playground to the edge of town, where the culvert runs beneath the motorway and becomes my realm. They're on the town-side. Maybe they instinctively recognise that this is the limit of where they have dominance; for all I know they actually piss up the concrete to mark their territory. Maybe just because it's better lit, which makes it a lot easier for me to sneak up on them from the echoing black throat of the underpass. I can see quite well in the dark as virtually anything other than Boy, but the irony is that I need my hands so can't do this as anything else, so I have to be very careful.

It's muddy and wet in here, litter strewn ankle-deep and stinking of silt, rot and piss. They come here to drink, do noz, weed, whatever, and on the rare occasion when they can convince girls to join them, fuck clumsily up against the stained concrete walls.

And apparently, I'm the one with the problem.

There are four of them. Not many, but then it is a school night. Aidan and three others I don't know. Flapper and Freckles, obviously too young for such manly exploits, must have gone home. Good thing.

Whatever I think of them, they're still Sean's mates and I wouldn't want them to be involved in what's about to happen. This is not a subtle plan, but then Aidan doesn't deserve anything more sophisticated.

He's in the middle of saying something hilarious, and probably completely untrue, about what he did to some girl and why she's a total slut when I fling a handful of fox shit that smacks him in the back of the head.

The moment freezes, beautiful, like a ballet dancer poised mid-pirouette.

Fox scat smells so bad because of their scavenging diet, and it has a thick, musky stench that's almost impossible to get rid of. I've seen dog walkers horrified and disgusted when their furry best friends have found some and decided to roll around in it, which, apart from anything else, just proves how stupid dogs are. It's also sticky, almost oily, and I watch, biting my lip in glee, as Aidan's fingers wander around to the back of his head and return smeared with brown-black shit.

He squeals. *Actually* squeals, a high pitched *eeeeeeee!!!* like a cartoon of a little old lady seeing a mouse. One of his mates begins to laugh, and then the others join in, and this is a hundred times more humiliating.

Aidan peers into the tunnel and sees me because I let him. It's important that he doesn't think Sean has anything to do with this, and I'd have been blamed even if he hadn't seen me, so I have nothing to lose. Plus, I like that he sees me; I want to rub his nose in it, in every possible sense.

His squeal deepens into a bellow of rage and he lunges for me.

I don't need hands anymore.

As Rat I outdistance him easily, scampering up and along the underpass wall to avoid getting bogged down in the muck on the ground. I could escape, but there's a point to be made here. A lesson he needs to learn.

The lane that becomes the Trod is hedged on either side—thick walls of holly and hawthorn, dense and loaded with spikes. I slip through and come up in the field on the other side as Boy, just as Aidan comes stomping and swearing along the lane I've just left. He can't see me, doesn't know where I've gone, is charging around in an unthinking rage, so I'm going to have to help him.

"Hey Aidan!" I call.

He whirls around. "Where are you, you little fucker?" he yells. I can smell the stink of him from here, even with a human nose. His three musketeers catch up, no doubt looking forward to seeing him feed me my own teeth.

"Here boy!" I whistle as you would to a dog, and wave. They see me now.

"How did he get over there?" says one of his mates.

"I don't give a fuck!" Aidan snarls. "Just find a way through!" He turns back to me and through the barrier of branches he says: "You. Are. So. Fucking. Dead."

There is a gate about twenty yards back up the track—coincidentally, the one that the new teacher used to turn around in—which they'll find soon, so I don't have much time.

"I watch you walk to school along here every day, Aidan," I say.

"So fucking what?" He's pacing back and forth along the hedge directly opposite me, testing it for gaps.

"So unless you fancy going to school every morning stinking of shit, you lay off Sean."

"Sean Curran? What the fuck has this got to do with him?"

"He's going up to Big School next year. You'll be in the Fifth Form. Lay off him. And his mates, Mike and Craig."

Aidan starts to shove his way through the hedge. There's no way he can do it, the thick branches are like iron bars and he's going to cut himself to shreds, but he's doing it anyway. "I don't know..." he grunts, twisting and pulling, "...if you're a homo..." *shove, grunt snap*,

"...or just a fucking retard..." *twist, shove*, "...but I'm going to kick the fucking shit out of you just the same."

I think I've touched a nerve.

I let some Fox snarl into my voice and say: "There are worse things that can happen to a person walking home from school on his own than having shit chucked at him, Aidan. Much worse."

That makes him pause. I think he's genuinely uncertain, maybe even afraid.

Then from my right one of his pack shouts, "Oy! There's a gate here!" and I hear heavy metal clambering sounds and know it's time to go.

As Rabbit, I streak away through the long grass at the base of the hedge, following the lane up into the Trod, where I am safe, and make the rest of the way to my lair as Boy. I tell myself that's sorted him out. I desperately want to tell Sean what happened—or anyone, for that matter—so that I can share the transcendent joy of that frozen moment when Aidan knew that something terrible had just happened to him but didn't know exactly what, but I can't, obviously.

Instead, I kill a few more hours until I judge it's past midnight, grab my things and head out to the motorway embankment.

It's a Lot Harder to Decapitate a Badger Than You Think

Mr Frederick's field ends at a tall security fence topped with barbed wire, and on the other side of it is the steeply wooded slope of the embankment. Brambles and nettles have been left to grow wild on the other side, crowding close, more effective than any man-made barrier in preventing trespassers from getting onto land which I assume is owned by the Highways Agency, or something like that. This has attracted lots of furry inhabitants who don't mind a bit of noise in return for not being actively shot or trapped.

Obviously, these barriers don't stop anyone who *really* wants to get up there, but the usual gaps and holes are too well-known and I can't risk being seen, so I need to find another way. That's why I brought the pliers, because of the wire-cutting blades just behind the main grip.

It's been raining, and I listen to the deep rumble of lorries and the higher hiss of car tyres a hundred metres ahead. There are floodlights along this stretch, since it's close to town, but not much illumination filters through the dense undergrowth. Satisfied that I am unlikely to be either seen or heard, I cut a two-foot vertical slit in the fence wire and bend the edges back. I don't mind brambles and nettles; I'm used to them by now. I could avoid them if I went through as Rabbit, but I need to carry the sack and shovel.

One time, me and Sean saw the aftermath of a traffic pile-up. It was a foggy afternoon on the Easter Bank Holiday and we'd been playing jungle warfare when we heard a sudden loud, crunching, shattering sound, followed by the squealing of tyres and several smaller collisions one after the other.

He looked at me with wide eyes. "That sounded like a smash-up!" he said. "Do you think anyone's dead?"

"Let's go see!" I shouted and we ran for the scene.

What had happened was obvious. Bank Holiday traffic, cars too close together, foggy conditions, somebody hits the brakes and the cars behind don't have room to stop. Multiple prangs, half a dozen vehicles all rear-ending each other like a huge, grinding, metal concertina.

"God, it's like the Human Centipede!" Sean gasped, staring at it. "Only with cars!" We were safely behind the crash barrier at the side, screened by bushes.

"The Human What?"

"It's this really stupid gross film," he says.

There was broken glass everywhere, in those glittering cubes like diamonds, and people stumbling around, crying. One woman was being sick out of a van window. A dozen metres from where Sean and me hid, a man sat on the roadside—just sat there with his legs out in front of him, his face and upper body covered in blood, and wearing what I thought was a weird kind of flat cap until I saw it was a big flap of his scalp, torn and hanging over his ear.

"What if something blows up?" I whispered to Sean.

"Don't be stupid," he said. "That only happens in films."

"Well excuse me, mister accident expert person."

Neither of us considered trying to help. We'd only have made things worse and gotten into trouble, so we watched until the ambulances and police turned up and then legged it because it was only a matter of time before somebody saw us, and even though nobody had caught us for the stone-throwing thing we still felt guilty, as if the consequences of our stupidity had only been deferred and this was somehow all our fault. The thing with guilt is, I must have done something very wrong for the Greenfather to have rejected me all these years, but you either let it paralyse you or you go ahead anyway. I've tried being paralysed for twelve years and where has that gotten me?

It's not as if I'm planning to kill a person. I'm not a monster.

I know there's a big badger sett on the top of the embankment, four dark holes big enough for a small child to crawl into surrounded by spoil heaps from the burrowing. But I'm not going down there—I'm not going anywhere near it as Boy. I creep towards it as Rabbit, and instantly I can see them: seven badgers rootling around in the undergrowth. Long snouts with white stripes up the sides, thickly muscled bodies. This strategy does not come without its risks, as badgers are omnivorous and have been known to eat rabbits (along with pretty much anything smaller than themselves), and when I hop into the middle of them I think they're too surprised to get all munchy because they just stop and stare at me, their long muzzles twitching as if to say, *What is this small, defenceless and edible creature doing amongst us?* One of them starts to waddle towards me.

I drop my Rabbit shape and stand up as Boy, waving my arms and shouting, "Boogah boogah boogah!"

The badgers scatter.

They run for their holes, grunting in alarm, but I've got between several of them and the sett and they flee from me, towards the motorway. I single one out and let the other two go, zigging and zagging as it turns and tries to get behind me, and I'm making so much noise that it's more scared of me than the bright lights of the carriageway, and then it's scooting under the guard rail and into traffic.

I stop, pull back into the bushes and watch.

It doesn't take long.

The badger freezes in the middle of the outside lane, stunned by light and noise. A blue car blares past, swerving to miss it, but the sixteen-wheel lorry after it doesn't have the manoeuvrability. There's a sound like a side of ham hitting a gong and the badger flies, spinning, caught for a moment in the truck's headlights before landing with a heavy thump on the hard shoulder to my left and sliding through the gravel for a short distance. It fetches up against one of the crash barrier uprights, motionless, and the truck ploughs on without stopping.

I can't believe my luck. I'd been afraid that the animal would run, or be flung, into the faster moving traffic of the inside lanes where it might have caused an accident or, worse still, become too mangled to use. Compared to some of the other ways badgers are killed—guns, dogs, poison—this was merciful. At least it was quick.

That said, the impact was obviously traumatic. The badger's guts are sticking out of its mouth and arsehole, and one of its eyes is gone, leaving a raw, bloody socket. No idea where that's got to. Maybe it's staring at the truck driver through his windscreen. That'd be pretty funny. The smell of its death is thick: blood, shit, and whatever's leaking out of its innards.

I have to wait until there's a lull in the traffic, so I won't be seen dragging the dead badger into the bushes, and that's where it gets tricky because it's a lot heavier than expected. Badgers are thickly muscled burrowing animals and there's no way I'm going to be able to drag this back to my lair, not even in a sack. I'm going to have to take its head off right here. I have a knife—only a tool, nothing like some of the town kids carry because they think it makes them look hard—just a few inches long. I've used it loads of times to gut fish and skin rabbits, so I tell myself that this is not much different, just a bit bigger.

Before I start, I place both hands on the animal's flank. It's still warm, and its hair is coarse. "Thank you, brother," I say. "Go in honour to the court of my father." I say this for every animal I have to kill, because it's just good manners.

Then I get started.

The soft stuff is easy, though with the blade being short I have to get right in there with my hands and it's slippery work. Nothing's spurting but it's hard to keep a good grip on the handle and I'm lucky that I don't cut my own fingers.

Then I get to the spine and I know that it's too much for my knife. I sit back on my heels and stare at the mess I've made. I'd thought that I could sort this out back at my lair; all I've got with me is the shovel, and I'm not too sure why I brought that. I'd imagined using it to scoop up the corpse and get it in the sack without having to touch it with my hands, but that's a moot point now. I'm covered in moot up to the elbows. I really haven't thought this through.

The shovel will have to do. The edge of the blade will be very blunt but there's no helping it.

I use it like an axe, aiming for the gash I've already made and hacking at it with variable accuracy. When I hit the spinal column it makes a very satisfying crunch, but when I miss and hit the mangled flesh either side it's like whacking a wet cushion with a cricket bat, and I can't avoid being splattered. Soon I'm dripping and my arms are burning from the effort, but with one final, hefty blow the head comes off and rolls to one side.

I take a moment, panting. I'm hot, sweaty, and covered in badger blood. Mama will go ballistic if she sees the state of me. Cars and trucks swish by just a few metres away, indifferent. I'm invisible to them. I might as well be in a different world as far as they're concerned.

When I've rallied a bit, I scoop the head into the sack and set off towards the Trod. Crows and red kites will take care of the carcass, and if anybody does find the remains no-one's going to bother about where its head is.

I wash off the worst of the muck in one of the little streams that runs off the steep side of Wickley Edge and when I'm feeling more myself, I head to the Sky Leaving Tree.

This is a big blackthorn that has been pollarded in the past, cut back so that its trunk stops about eight feet from the ground and then explodes outwards in a cluster of limbs. At the centre is a dense mass of twigs and leaf mulch that has built up over the years, like a massive nest. It's guarded by dozens of intertwined branches loaded with inch-long thorns, and it's impossible to reach unless you know where to put your hands, otherwise you can get badly stuck. This is where I put things that need to rot down before I can use them. Scavengers can eat their fill undisturbed, and it's high enough that the smell of decay won't attract human attention. I'd like to have the badger's skull as soon as possible, but it was messy enough work getting the bloody thing off in the first place and I'm not about to go skinning it and scooping out the brains and everything when I can just let the woods do the work for me. I've learned to be patient.

There's a mobile of tiny brass bells hanging from the inside of the back door so I can't get in without Mama hearing me, so I climb the back wall of the house to my bedroom window as usual. I open my door a crack and sniff. The sweet tang of weed drifts up from the ground floor and I know that Mama will be safe for a bit, so I scrub my hands in the bathroom, slip my fouled clothes into the washing machine on a quick cycle and go downstairs to snuggle up next to her on the sofa.

She hesitates in surprise before draping an arm over me.

"You're in a good mood," she says. "Did you have a good birthday?"

I squirm closer into her warmth and smell, a small burrowing creature. "Yes Mama," I say. "The best birthday ever."

The Book Booth

THE NEXT TIME LISA SAW WREN WAS THREE WEEKS later at morning break, watching the children play from the shadows of the trees on the other side of the schoolyard fence. It had been a church, once—St Luke's, sitting between the school and the rectory. On Lisa's early explorations of the village she had spotted a small notice board which said merely that it had suffered storm damage and been demolished in 1959, the graves relocated to the big municipal cemetery on the outskirts of the town, and the ground deconsecrated. Trees had reclaimed the churchyard long ago, but there were too many other properties nearby for it to be proper woodland. As far as anybody knew, the church still owned it and had never sold it for redevelopment, so it lingered in a semi-wild condition, a place for fly-tipping and making out, rumoured to be full of poachers' traps, or worse. It was strictly out of bounds for the students. That was where he was standing, not quite close enough to touch the wrought-iron railings.

A group of Year 6 boys had brought a foam rubber torpedo football that made a high-pitched screaming noise when it was thrown. One of them, either more enthusiastic or just less aware of his own strength, lobbed it high over his friends' heads and over the fence, where it disappeared amongst the trees to cries of dismay. It was as Lisa's eyes followed its trajectory that she saw the pale boy. Wren Collins.

He knew he'd been spotted. A moment later he was gone.

And a moment later he was back, holding the torpedo ball.

She held out her hand. He looked at the ball, clearly thinking of taking it for himself, but then he tossed it to her with pin-point precision. She caught it and raised a hand in thanks. He nodded, once, and was gone. This time he didn't come back.

The first time she spoke to him was in the first week of October. He'd been keeping a low profile; if he had been listening to story-time then it had been while hiding, most likely under her classroom window. Once, she'd gone out after the children had gone home to see if there was any sign of him, but she had no clue how to read the ground. An elephant could have been standing out there and she'd have been none the wiser—though she did find a scattering of small, curled wood shavings, the kind that might be produced by the sharpening of a pencil the old-fashioned way, with a pen-knife. The idea of Wren crouched below her window sharpening a stick while she prattled on about foxes and gingerbread men only made her feel more uneasy.

She met him in the place she'd least expected: the old telephone booth in the village. It was morning recess and she wasn't on playground duty so she'd popped to the shop for some stamps. Wren was sitting on a park bench, head down in an old paperback, the dark curtain of his fringe hanging over his face. His shorts were ragged cut-offs, his Transformers t-shirt grubby about the collar, and his bare feet were filthy as they kicked back and forth. On the ground beside him was a wicker hand-basket containing a loaf of bread and a newspaper. He was painfully thin, and he reminded her of old photographs of Depression-era urchins. And yet he was obviously and totally absorbed by what he was reading.

At the same time as her heart went out to the boy, the professional part of her was wondering exactly how well he could read. He wasn't being fed and clothed properly so it seemed unlikely he was getting a lot of story-time at home, and if he wasn't going to school either, then where was he learning it? Was he teaching himself?

Lisa tried to be nonchalant, opening the booth door and perusing the shelves without acknowledging that she'd seen him, and even though he didn't look up she could tell from the way that his feet stopped waggling that he was watching her.

"I like your name," she said, still without looking at him. She could have been talking to the books. "Is it Wren like the bird or Ren like the cartoon character?" He wouldn't have had a clue about Ren and Stimpy but that wasn't the point.

It took him such a long time to reply that if she hadn't known better she'd have thought that he had either hearing difficulties or some kind of intellectual impairment.

"Bird," he murmured. At least he'd answered, not just run off. Then: "Troglodytes," he added, pronouncing it *trog-lo-die-tees.*

"I beg your pardon?" She looked at him now and saw his eyes glittering at her just like they had in the classroom—watchful, alert, like an animal ready to bolt.

"Their Greek name," he said. "Troglodytes. Means lives in caves."

"Why yes, it does."

"That's a joke. It's ironic."

"Is it?"

But he clearly wasn't going to explain it. He closed his book, slid off the bench and stood peering past her into the booth, book clutched tightly in both hands. His gaze shifted to her. "I need to put this back," he said.

She realised that she was blocking his way. "Oh, right. Sorry." And stepped aside.

He slipped past her with the slow caution of a half-tamed creature, and this close the smell of him was sharp and pungent; he obviously hadn't had a decent wash in weeks. As he reached out and put his book back in the gap where it had come from she saw, with a sick cold feeling in her stomach, a ladder of white scars climbing the brown skin up the back of his forearm. *Jesus, he's cutting himself?* Then he slipped out again, watching her every second of the way.

"Things have to go back where they belong," he said.

And where do you belong, Wren-with-a-W, my little troglodyte boy? she wanted to ask, but it would have been too much too soon. He was certainly pale enough to be living an underground existence. No wonder the other kids called him Gollum, poor thing.

He picked up his basket and took off across the road, through a gap in the hedgerow, and was gone.

"Bye then," she said, watching him go. Then she looked back at the book he'd replaced, and took it off the shelf. "*The Sleepers of Else*, is it? This is what you're reading?" The book was so old that there wasn't even a barcode on the back. The cover was a strange montage of what looked like heavily filtered photography and seventies prog rock album art: a spreading tree with a knight asleep at its foot and huge freakish owl eyes filling the sky behind. When she opened it she saw that the pages faded from cream to caramel at the edges, and the sweet dry smell of it reminded her, for some reason, of biscuit tins. She put it in her bag to read later. Who knew? Maybe it would give some insights into how his mind worked—or at least something in common to talk about.

Mama's New Project, and Mine

FROM THE TREES I WATCH THE NEW TEACHER LEAVE the Book Booth. I don't know how I feel about the conversation we've just had. The robin's-egg courtier said that she wasn't to be trusted, but all the same I feel a bit guilty now for trying to get her stuck in the Deep Trod.

When I get home, Mama has a ladder against the side of the house and she's halfway up it. She's still in the clothes that she was wearing when she fell asleep on the sofa last night, to which she has added wellington boots and bright yellow washing up gloves, and she's digging in the gutters with what looks like a serving spoon. At some point between dispatching me to the shop and now she's obviously decided to start a new project, and got it fixed in her head that the gutters need cleaning right now. She'll be at this project without stopping until it's done, or until the notion leaves her. She gets them every six months or so and I suppose we're overdue, or it could just be the aftermath of my birthday. One time, her project was to repaint the house—which, to be fair to her, did need doing—but it's a big house and she decided to do it single-handedly and the notion left her before the project could be completed, which is why the ground floor is nice and new-looking while the top two look like something out of a horror film. But the gutters look like a much smaller project; she might get this one finished. The problem is that she won't sleep or eat, which means her temper is likely to turn just like that.

I try to do a subtle about-face but it's no good, she heard the back gate rattle when I opened it.

"Wren?" she calls. "Is that you?"

"Yes, Mama." I scurry across the lawn for the back door.

"Where have you been? You've been ages!"

"Sorry, Mama. Just getting bread and the newspaper like you asked."

"Oh, so it's my fault now, is it?" She digs into the gutter with her spoon, levers out a black clot of encrusted filth and flings it at me, but her aim is terrible and I dodge in through the back door. "Cheeky little shit!" she yells after me.

I chuck the bread and paper onto the kitchen counter as I run through without stopping and into the hall towards the front door, wondering if I have enough food at my lair to last for however long this project lasts, and hoping that she won't have had time to get down the ladder yet, but of course it's locked and when I fumble it open she's there. Her speed always surprises me.

"I asked you where you've been," she says. "The question was not rhetorical." Her eyes are wide and dark and jittery, like she's eaten deadly nightshade again.

"Just to the shop, Mama, I promise. I stopped for a bit of a read at the Book Booth but it wasn't long, honest." I could deflect her anger—and it's not anger, really, just that dark jittery stuff overspilling into something very similar—by saying that the new teacher delayed me, but sometimes with Mama it's worse if you try to put the blame on someone else. Better to take the responsibility, and your punishment, like the princeling you are. "I swear it won't happen again."

"You're bloody right it won't." Fast, *so* fast, the big plastic spoon lashes out and finds my ear in a burst of pain like a nail's just been hammered into it, and my head is full of ringing on that side. "Do you have any idea how much work there is to be done?" she demands. "Winter's coming, and the gutters need cleaning and I want to get water tanks on each of the down-pipes, not to mention the state of the roof tiles. I want you up there clearing off that moss by nightfall! Honestly, the state of this place! So much time and energy wasted on trying to get the Greenfather to pay any attention to you, but since he obviously doesn't give a shit you may as well make yourself useful around here a bit more instead of wasting your time reading and buggering off to play in the woods . . ."

She wanders away, waving her spoon and ranting, and soon I hear the metallic creak of her footsteps on the ladder. I consider legging it, but decide against. I definitely don't have the provisions to wait this out, and the last thing I want is her thrashing around through the trees looking for me. She doesn't know about the lair—nobody does, not even Sean, and I mean to keep it that way.

So for the next couple of days I'm a good boy. I check on the badger skull, collect what I need from the woods, and try to keep out of everybody's way.

I mean, I really do try. What happens next isn't my fault.

Rambling

On the morning after her encounter with Wren at the Book Booth, Lisa found an intricately woven bundle of feathers and twigs outside on the windowsill by her classroom desk. She took this to be a gesture of welcome from him, and felt oddly as if he had given her permission to explore the village in more detail.

She started to spend her free weekends exploring the woods. As October faded into November she ranged north, past where Edge Lane ended at a small parking space for ramblers' cars and became a national walking trail called the Edge Way. In the Book Booth she found a small guide to identifying native trees, and taught herself to spot ash, hawthorn, birch and oak. She wandered amongst the tangled lanes that she'd only ever driven through before—Spinney Lane, Whitcombe Lane—and tried to get a sense of who lived here and how.

Some of the houses were tidy and clean, nestled behind thick hedges and wrought-iron gates—the kinds of places bought by senior barristers and surgical consultants and minor sporting celebrities. Expensive cars appeared in their driveways on the weekend and were gone during the week, because these weren't homes for such people, they were getaways. Their money was spent in towns and cities, and when they went out to the Hanged Man for a drink they could be heard consoling with the locals about how terrible it was that there was so little in such a lovely place. Many of the houses owned by the locals, who themselves were mostly well over retirement age, were in more serious need of attention, with sagging rooflines, peeling window frames and gardens overrun by the surrounding woodland. When Lisa finally located Wren's home, she wasn't surprised to see that it was the worst of the bunch.

Her one attempt to meet his mother did not go well.

She pressed the doorbell and heard it jangle somewhere deep inside. Then she waited. The front door was old and wooden, its deep green paint cracked and peeling, and set in the middle of it was a stained-glass panel depicting intertwined roses that had a wedge-shaped chip missing and a yellowing piece of sticky tape covering the gap. To either side of the front porch, untended hydrangea bushes swarmed at large sash windows, the big globes of their flower-heads ragged and spilling wilted handfuls of petals like confetti, filling the still air with the sweet reek of their rot. Where the bushes could not conquer, the ivy took over, scrambling up between, and in some cases over, the windowpanes, searching for the guttering that hung askew three storeys above. Several panes were broken, patched with plastic carrier bags. If she had not been told that people lived here, she would have sworn that it was abandoned. There were no lights visible inside, though it appeared that heavy drapes blinded every window, and it was all too easy to imagine unfriendly eyes peering down at her from between mildewed curtains.

There was no car or vehicle of any kind in the driveway, and even that was hard to make out: a gravelled strip leading from the lane to a pair of sagging wooden garage doors that was just a bit less overgrown than the rest of the front garden—or what passed for one. The knee-high grass was not just overgrown, it was actively rewilding, with hazel and hawthorn saplings springing out of what must once have been lawn, though no lawnmower had seen this for at least a decade. Here and there she saw, half-hidden in clumps and tussocks, the remains of old plastic children's toys—a tricycle, a slide, a seesaw—but so bleached by years of exposure that they were pale, like bones in an untended graveyard.

Across the garage doors some vandal had spray-painted *Fuck off witch whore!* in jagged black letters. An attempt had been made to paint over it, but the words were clear.

It must once have been a handsome house, she thought. The kind of place that even in its state of semi-dereliction would fetch an asking price way out of her league. How could anyone let a place like this fall into such a condition? Come to that, how could anyone who seemed to be so poverty-stricken as Wren's mother afford somewhere like it in the first place?

She rang the doorbell again, and heard that distant, discordant jangle.

She was wrong. There was nobody in. This had been a stupid idea anyway. She put the parcel that she'd brought with her down in front of the door, hoping that it would speak for itself, and turned to go.

Footsteps on a wooden floor inside, rattle of chains and drawing of bolts, and the door was dragged open, scraping.

"What do you want?"

Up close, Lisa's first impression was that Wren's mother was a lot younger than she'd been expecting, barely older than herself. She must have been only just out of her teens when she'd become a mother. She was wearing a shapeless brown jumper, camouflage-print trousers and sheepskin boots. An early autumn chill edged the air, and to judge from the house's exterior it was a safe bet that they didn't have central heating. Like her son, there was a pallor to her skin and a bruised look about the eyes that made Lisa think she was talking to someone suffering a consumptive disease.

"Fine, sod off then," she said, and started to close the door.

"No, wait! Sorry! I didn't mean to stare."

The door paused. "Well, what did you mean, then?"

Lisa gestured at the parcel lying by the door. "It's, well, I suppose it's a sort of present. For your boy. If that's all right, obviously."

"Oh, obviously." Wren's mother peered down at the parcel as if it might be a bomb. It was about the size of a brick, wrapped in brown paper and secured with rubber bands.

"It's books," said Lisa. "For Wren. I met him at the Book Booth a while ago and, well, I gather he likes to read, so. They're mine. I mean they're old ones of mine, from when I was a girl. I thought he might like them."

"Oh, you did, did you? Did you think they might *bring him out of himself a bit*? Or that they might *boost his re-engagement with learning*? Did you think that they would *enhance his literacy*?"

The venom in her voice took Lisa by surprise. "That's not what I—"

"I know exactly who you are. You're that new teacher. Simon Blake's replacement. Temporary, aren't you, until they find someone proper? He didn't have any luck with Wren and he bloody lived here—what chance do you think you stand, swanning in in the morning in your nice little car and then swanning out again afterwards?"

"I'm just trying to—"

"Back to your nice little house and your nice little boyfriend..."

"Look, I don't want anything from your boy, all right?" She was stung by the other woman's instant and unprovoked aggression. "I just thought it might be a nice gesture for a kid who's obviously very lonely. But fine, if you don't want it, sod you." She snatched up the package. "And no, you don't know the first thing about me."

"Exactly!" she heard the other woman shout as she stormed off through the pigsty of a yard, face burning. "So why would I take anything from you?"

◆ ◆ ◆

On the plus side, Lisa was able to get a good look at the Trod in daylight, which put at least one nightmarish experience into perspective.

"Inosculation," she read, "is a natural phenomenon in which trunks, branches, or roots of two trees grow together, join, and become a single organism."

She closed the little book and looked up. High above, two oaks—their ancient boles as thick as temple columns, their bark as gnarled as elephant hide—rose from the sandstone banks on either side of the holloway, which were themselves already well above head height, and their lowest limbs met in an arch exactly like that of a cathedral. From that apex hung a length of rope, its end broken and frayed. She told herself that it was almost certainly the remains of an old swing that the local kids had used once upon a time, but it was all too easy to imagine the figure of a man hanging with his feet bumping and slithering over the roof of her car—dead toes that were black and swollen with coagulated blood, but which nevertheless scratched and stretched...

Fear flooded her and she turned to run.

Then she swallowed it and stayed where she was. *No you don't,* she thought. *You scared me off once, and fair play to you, but not a second time. You're just a bloody tree.*

A dark crimson oak leaf seesawed lazily down to land amongst the roots at her feet. The roots were as thick as human limbs at the top of the sandstone banks, and they looped and curled down through the face of each bank, becoming thinner and more serpentine until they enmeshed themselves with each other in a frenzied tangle underfoot at the deepest point of the Trod, so that both oaks formed an unbroken circuit from root to leaf and it was impossible to tell where one finished and the other started.

Though the air in the Trod was still—close and somehow

oppressive, like an indrawn breath—there must have been a breeze higher up because the branches slowly writhed against one another, whispering as they did so. Another blood red leaf spiralled down, and as her eyes rose to trace its origin she saw that she was utterly wrong. There was no breeze up there.

Wren was creeping amongst the upper branches, some of them surely too thin to support even his under-nourished weight, placing his long-fingered hands carefully, then shifting his feet one at a time. He was naked and covered in filth from head to foot so that his pale skin didn't show up so clearly in the dimness.

He was stalking her.

You're not supposed to see him. If you see him you have to pretend that you didn't otherwise he gets scared and runs away.

She drew in a deep breath and let it out very slowly, then turned and retraced her steps back up the holloway to light and sanity, trying to betray no sign that she knew he was there or that inwardly she was cringing at every rustle and twitch of foliage, convinced that he was right above her and about to drop onto her head like a massive spider. Then she saw the red post-box at the top gleaming like a rescue buoy, and abandoned her forced nonchalance to stride the last dozen yards and actually grasped hold of it in relief. She chanced a glance upwards and back at the trees of the Trod, but there was no sign of him, if he had even been there at all.

How Sean and Me Invented Badger Skull Jet-wash Football

I'VE BEEN CHECKING ON THE BADGER SKULL EVERY FEW days and the signs are promising—a lot of the flesh has been taken by birds and scavengers, and what's left is covered in maggots—but the process is so slow. If I had six months, I could let it weather properly to the right kind of bone whiteness, but I just don't have that kind of luxury, not if I'm going to get any answers before the frost comes and the Greenfather takes his winter aspect and turns cruel. I'm going to have to take matters into my own hands, quite literally, and I'm not looking forward to it. If I try to boil the stinking thing in the kitchen, Mama might actually kill me, and anyway, I'm not sure it would even fit in her largest pot. Plus, then I'd have to explain what I need a skull that big for.

But it's all right, Sean's parents have something even better.

"So," I say, all casual, as we're walking back from school one day. "Do you reckon your dad will let you borrow the jet-washer?"

Sean's dad has got one of those high-pressure jet-washer things that you plug your garden hose into, and a compressor powered from the mains. It has a business end that looks like a mediaeval jousting lance with a pistol grip that sprays water in a thin jet with such force that it can take the mortar out from between bricks. Don't ask me how I know. He uses it to clean off his mountain bike after he's been on one of his off-road adventures, and he takes ages. I've seen mothers wash their babies with less care—though admittedly not with a jet-washer. That would be sick and wrong.

"I don't know," says Sean. "I'll ask him. What do you want to use it for?"

There's no point trying to lie to him about this. "I want to use it to hose the rotting flesh off a dead badger's skull." I see no value in telling him how I obtained the head.

Sean looks at me. "Cool," he says.

And that's how we invent the game of badger skull jet-wash football.

◆ ◆ ◆

Sean tells his dad that he wants to earn some pocket money for Christmas, which is exactly the sort of go-getting enterprise that Chris likes to see in young people, and fair play to Sean, he's never going to win a Nobel Prize, but he does know which of his dad's buttons to push.

The deal is, if Sean can clear the moss and weeds off the drive by the time his mum and dad get back after picking up his little sister from the child-minder, he'll earn a tenner, which gives him and me about an hour of uninterrupted experimentation time.

We take the skull in a plastic bag, stinking to high heaven, into his back yard and he plugs the jet-washer in, uncoiling hoses and electrical cables while I tip the bag's contents onto the lawn. It might have been noted that I have a tendency not to think things through. Sean, for his part, and being the easy-going mate that he is, tends to let me have my head when it comes to our joint adventures. I can be a bit of a bully if I don't get my way.

He switches on the compressor, which rattles into life. The hose is making an alarming hissing noise and water is squirting out of the joints where he's screwed the lance to it.

"Are you sure that's on properly?" I ask.

He peers at it. "Dunno," he says, and offers it to me. "Want to go first?"

I am feeling magnanimous, and more importantly don't want to be holding this thing when it catastrophically disassembles, as seems likely, so I say no, it's his toy, he can play with it first.

Sean strikes a swaggering, wide-legged stance for stability, aims the lance, and clutches the pistol grip.

It does not catastrophically disassemble. All the same, it hasn't occurred to either of us that we should have secured the head to the ground in some way. Instead, with a tremendous PHWOOSH! like a volcanic geyser erupting, a seething white line of high-pressure water blasts from the end of the lance and hits the badger's head square on, sending it tumbling across the lawn like a football and into the rhododendron bushes at the bottom.

Sean and I look at each other, eyes shining, and the game is afoot.

The head comes out of the bushes minus its lower jaw but that's all right because I only need the main skull to make a mask. I was afraid that it would simply disintegrate, and that might have happened if I'd left it longer to go brittle, but as it is the bone is fresh enough to stand up to the water. We designate two trees as goalposts and take it in turns; points are scored for the fewest number of squirts needed to get the "ball" between them. Sean is ahead four points to two when he looks at the swamp that the lawn is turning into and calls full time.

We need to get the job done. We need to brace the head against something, so we put it up against the back wall of the garage.

This turns out to be a bad idea, because the jet of water hits the skull, sloughing off more of the filth, and then rebounds and covers us in a cloud of water, mud, and rotting flesh.

There's a certain amount of swearing.

Afterwards, we look at the mess—the sodden lawn, scarred where the high-pressure jet has torn chunks out of the grass—and I say, "You can tell your parents that this was my idea, if you like."

"This *was* your idea!" he shouts.

"Yeah," I say. "Probably best not to mention the skull, all the same."

"I'm going to do the drive," he mutters, shouldering the lance and squelching off around the side of the house.

I take that as my cue to leave.

◆ ◆ ◆

Collateral damage aside, the jet-wash has done the trick: the soft tissues have been scoured away and all that's left are a few stubborn shreds of fur and sinew that I can take care of by the more traditional method of boiling and then going at it with a wire brush.

Without the lower jaw (which we couldn't find despite searching intensely for at least several minutes), it fits snugly in Mama's big soup pan, where it sits on a rolling boil for a quarter of an hour before she comes into the kitchen to see what's making the smell.

Instead of having a go, she seems to be pleased. "That's a beauty," she says, peering into the pan and nodding approval. "Where did your father leave this for you?"

"By the motorway," I say. I want to add *But he didn't leave it for me. I took it, just like I'm going to take everything else that is my birthright*, but I don't. That's not an argument I want to have right now.

She's right though, it is beautiful. Denuded of flesh, it's easy to see how long and sharp the incisors are, curved and shining. It's rounder than a fox's skull, with a prominent ridge running over it like a crest.

"It's going to look wonderful," she continues, and I wonder how much of this uncharacteristically chummy tone of hers is because she's afraid that I'm still angry with her.

“I’m going to my room to have a read,” I say. “I’ll be back to check on it in ten minutes.”

I leave her watching the skull which is rocking to and fro gently with the motion of the water, like it’s eager to get going.

Fair Play to Aidan, He Knows Which Buttons to Push

WITH EVERYTHING ELSE GOING ON I'VE COMPLETELY forgotten about Aidan, which turns out to be a terrible oversight.

I smell the smoke first.

It's the early hours of the morning and I'm investigating an abandoned rabbit burrow as Rat, looking for bones, when I come back to the surface and it hits me. As Boy I might not have noticed it until much later, so at least I have some warning. I know woodsmoke. I know the sweet scent of burning apple wood, the heavy sharpness of holly, the rich earthiness of oak—all, in their proper time and place, are good smells. This is none of those. This stinks like burning piss, if piss could burn, and the corrosive stench of it feels like acid in my sensitive rodent's nose. I have to check an almost overwhelming compulsion to flee back underground as far and as deep as I can to escape it.

It's petrol, burning.

My first thought is the motorway, that there's been an accident and this time the thing that Sean and I feared has actually happened: a vehicle has caught fire and someone will be trapped and dying in the worst possible way. Then I realise that the wind's in the wrong direction for that. This smell is coming from the village, and now there's a crisp brown undertone to it which hits me with a jolt of recognition like a brick in the face, snaps me back into Boy and sets me running for the source of it—running barefoot over sharp sticks and rocks but not feeling them—running and moaning *no-no-no* because I know what that brown smell is that's worse than petrol and worse than burning flesh: it's book paper.

Through the trees the Book Booth looks like an old-fashioned lantern. The silhouette of its rectangular panels frames the yellow glow from inside. Except closer up it's not so much a glow as a raging inferno. Everything inside is on fire, all of it, the books flapping and twisting like dying birds. Above the roaring I hear pops and cracks as the glass panels shatter, and from them spews flame and smoke and glowing, floating, lacy red embers of burning paper.

I am frozen with the horror of it, or the beauty, I can't tell, until I see him standing on the other side of the road, half-hidden by the trees, watching his handiwork. He's wearing one of those hoodies that zips up all the way over his face and makes a zombie mask, but I know that it's Aidan.

I howl and charge at him, too enraged to do it as anything, which is another in a long line of my stupid mistakes. Because he's bigger than me, isn't he? The only things I've got going for me as Rat or Fox are speed and teeth, neither of which I currently have. He sees me coming, could run, doesn't, instead reaches out almost casual-like with an arm that happens to end in a fist, and I fold around it like his fist is a black hole. Winded, sucking vacuum, I collapse and squirm at his feet.

His voice is close to my ear: "I thought I was going to have to tell people that I saw you do it. Now I don't even have to do that. Cheers, freak." He kicks me in the guts, more as an afterthought, I think, because I'm already so clenched around the void of my stomach that it doesn't make much difference. Lying on my side, retching, I see him run away at ninety degrees to the world.

I roll over and get to my knees, hugging myself. Smoke stings my eyes. Bonfire heat washes me.

Other voices now, shouts of alarm coming from the direction of the pub:

"What in God's name…?"

"How did…"

"Is that Wren?"

The light of a torch bounces as someone comes running towards me, then its glare is in my face. I've made it to my knees by this point. I could tell them who did it but they wouldn't believe me. Aidan could be standing with a petrol canister in one hand and a lighted match in the other and they'd still think it was me if he said so. I get nothing from being found like this except a beating to add to the blame which is already mine, so I do the only thing I can, which is to run for the safety of the darkness under the trees as more lights and voices join the chorus.

"That's Wren!"

"It was Wren!"

"There he goes!"

"What the fuck have you done now, Gollum?"

What indeed.

◆ ◆ ◆

I spend the rest of the night in hiding. I hear sirens, and voices in the woods shouting my name—voices of men I don't recognise, punctuated by the squawk and crackle of police radios. When the noise dies down, I make Kevin and send him to check if the coast is clear. I consider going myself as Mouse or something equally small and sneaky, but my nerves are so rattled that I honestly don't trust my self-control.

Kevin seems to have regained some of his antic jester spirits, and he toddles off with a brisk "Cheerio!" as if my misfortune has cheered him up mightily. I think I'm going to have to do something about Kevin at some point. He takes somewhat longer than necessary to come back and tell me that the police have gone, and I'm not sure that I can completely trust him, but I have no choice—he's the only twigger I can make without having to quicken it at the Greenfather Oak.

Warier than any mouse, I creep home through woodland shrouded ankle-deep in early morning mist.

Mama is chopping firewood in the back yard. I hang back in the treeline and watch through one of the gaps in the fence. This is one of my jobs. We don't have central heating, and she says that she's not paying through the nose for electricity when the Greenfather provides what we need for free, so in the early autumn it's my job to forage and chop enough wood to see us right for fires through the winter. Why is she doing my job? I don't do hers.

Maybe she thinks I'm not coming back.

I break cover and climb through the fence, stopping just on the other side and well out of axe range.

She pauses on the upswing, glances at me, grunts, "Oh there you are," and continues with the downstroke. The block of wood splits with a *chonk!* "I had the pigs here looking for you. Told them to bugger off but I think they'll be back with a warrant."

"I didn't do it, Mama!" I blurt.

"Of course you didn't," she says, kicks the split pieces to one side and lines up another block. "You, burning those books? Only an idiot would think you'd do that."

"But they all do!"

She lines up the axe. "Yes, well, that's because they're all idiots."

Chonk!

As if she's hacked something free in me, I burst into tears and run to her, fling my arms around her and press myself to her bosom. She's wearing her big brown jumper, and she smells of wool and wood smoke and cigarettes and beer—mother smell. I'm a sobbing mess again, all tears and snot, and a small, detached part of me thinks that I really need to get a handle on all this blubbing. It's not like me at all. She endures this for a moment, then her hand comes up and for a silly moment I think it's going to rest on my head but instead it curls around my shoulder and pulls me off her.

"Are you done?" she asks. "Have you finished feeling sorry for yourself?" Her eyes search me, not unloving, but as implacable as the axe.

I nod, wiping my nose on my sleeve.

"Good," she says. "Because the only question is what are you going to do about it?"

"What can I do? They'll never believe me, no matter what I say!"

"You're right there, they won't. You'll never change their minds. But I'm not talking about them. I'm talking about *him*. The one that did it. What are you going to do about *him*? What is the son of the Greenfather going to do to punish those that would cross him?"

"There's nothing I can do! He's bigger than I am!"

She leans on the axe and inspects me. "Bigger, yes. Stronger. But only *here*." She grasps one of my scrawny upper arms. "You are strong in other places. What makes *you* strong?"

She's right. I'm thinking like a human child. I need to get a handle on that, too.

"The Trod," I reply.

"Then use that. Use it to show people what happens when they cross us. Show your father who you really are. And then we'll both put on our nicest smiles for the authorities and you're going to convince them that you're just a strange but basically harmless little boy with a good mother who loves and cares for you."

"And what if I can't? What if they don't believe me?"

"Then I'll have no choice but to tell them about your secret hiding place and all the nasty things you keep there. They'll lock you up and throw away the key."

My gasp of horror must be comical, because she laughs. "Oh yes, my little princeling, I know all about your lair. I have done for years. I've got no objection to you skulking off and doing whatever it is that you do." I relax slightly, because it doesn't sound like she's actually been there and seen everything. "But if the police are going to find out what you are then they might as well find out everything, mightn't they?"

"Yes Mama," I mumble.

"So you be clever. Take your time and don't go off half-cocked; don't give them any reason to think it was you. You bide your time and pick the best moment, not the soonest."

She hasn't asked how I know who it is. She doesn't want to know who it is. She's not going to get involved, or help me. But that also means she's not going to interfere with what I do next.

It's a kind of love, I suppose.

How I Dealt With Aidan

THERE'S STILL PLENTY OF TIME BEFORE SCHOOL. IT'S possible that Aidan will bunk off today, but I think he'll want to keep up the pretence of innocence and avoid drawing attention to himself, so he'll stick to his routine. Which is good, because it gives me time to go back to the lair and get the stuff I need: my special flint knife and my birthday mask.

Opening the Greenfather Oak to the Deep Trod is not something to be done lightly. Most members of the Outer Courts have no interest in the human world, but there are enough of them scratching away on the other side of the air that you have to be very careful about how wide you open it and for how long. Some of them are just curious, but for others their curiosity runs along lines like *I wonder what this person's insides look like*, or *I wonder how long I can make them scream for*. So Mama and I wear the masks for camouflage.

I put mine on and the holly thorns settle reassuringly against the skin of my cheeks, nose, lips and forehead. The mask is good *because* of the thorns, not in spite of them, because they tell you instantly if your face accidentally frowns or smiles, they force you to be controlled—control your face, your movements and your thoughts—and control is really the only weapon you've got against what is waiting in the Deep Trod.

On my way to the holloway I pass close enough to Edge Lane to see the little crowd of people clustered around the burnt-out telephone booth. It used to be glossy red but now it's black and skeletal, dripping, broken panes of jagged shards grey with ash and the grass for a wide circle around it is seared and smeared with soot and scattered with sodden and half-burned books. A small group of villagers are moving around with bin bags and litter pickers, solemnly, like war crime investigators excavating a mass grave, not talking to each other. I see the new teacher there, too, and it looks like she's crying. I am seized by a sudden and absurd impulse to run over there and hug her and say yes, I know how you feel, but the holly mask stabs as my lips try to move on their own, reminding me of my priorities, and I squash that impulse. Time to get a handle on all of this.

The Trod, then.

With it being so sheltered, the trees of the holloway hang onto their autumn leaves longer than in other places, and the entire tunnel of it is blazing with pumpkin orange. It's like being swallowed by a throat of fire. It will be getting busy soon. Aidan's not the only one walking the old track into Stanton to get to school. I have to be quick and sneaky, and find a way to avoid involving innocent passers-by. I'm not a monster.

Although, says a sly little voice which sounds like it might be coming from the mask, *they all believe I did it so who gives a shit if someone else gets caught up?*

Because it might be Sean, or someone in his family. It might be the new teacher. She was *crying*.

I look up at the place where the large lower branches of the two oaks merge, the point of the arch, and the ragged length of rope that hangs there. If you ask anybody in the village about it, they'll tell you it's just where the local kids used to have a tyre-swing once upon a time, and that may be true, but I know what really used to swing there.

This is how to open the Deep Trod:

It takes blood, obviously, because blood powers everything. Climb to the top, where the lowest and biggest oak limbs have grown together. Cut yourself with the old flint knife and offer blood there, to the Court of the Sky. It can't be a steel knife because everybody knows that the dwimfolk don't like iron. Climb down the east-facing trunk to where it emerges from the rim of the holloway and offer blood to the Court of the Sun, then climb down, cross the holloway, climb back up the other side to the west trunk and offer blood to the Court of the Moon. Then slide back down the curving bank, just like one of those half-pipes where Aidan and his mates skate, to where the oak roots tangle together, and offer blood to the Court of the Earth. How far it opens depends on how much blood you offer. It's really very simple. I don't understand why people have to dress this up with things like candles and robes and crowns of flowers, as if anything from the Deep Trod is going to be impressed by that.

I stop short of offering to the Earth, find a thick root to hide behind, and wait.

After a few minutes a blackbird flutters down and starts flipping over leaves, looking for bugs. Then it scarpers when a tractor appears above the holloway on its way up past the village.

Nothing much happens for a while after that.

My stomach grumbles at the lack of breakfast.

I get excited when I hear footsteps further up the Trod, but it turns out to be just old Mr Fredericks on his usual morning stroll into town, and I almost decide that's it, I was wrong, Aidan isn't going to school today, he's pulling a sickie, when there he is.

Slouching along, staring at his phone, the tinny buzzing of something that sounds like wasps in his ears.

I stand in the middle of the Trod, right in his way, my bare feet amongst the snarled roots. I can feel the life in them, tingling against my toes: water and nutrients and fungi and bacteria passing back and forth, a battery circuit for the soul of this gate that just wants a little jump start to open. The air at my back seethes with the busy-ness which means that the Courts can sense something potent about to happen.

Blood trickles down my left arm, pooling in the hand that I hold cupped before my chest. Blood of the Greenfather.

"Hello Aidan," I say.

He can't possibly have heard me, but he must sense something in his path and he looks up from his phone. His eyes widen in surprise, just like the badger's did, and I have time to notice that there are dark circles under them as if he hasn't slept well, and I think maybe he feels guilty, maybe I should give him a second chance, but the mask stabs me as a reminder. And then he sneers.

"Fucksake, Gollum. What the fuck have you got on your face? Is that meant to scare me? There are worse things than fox shit I could meet walking to school? Is this it?" He laughs. "It's like you actually want me to beat the shit out of you. Because you know I'm always happy to. And your mate Sean, too."

"I told you, lay off him."

He laughs again. "Lay off him? I'll lay off him all right. I'll lay the fuck off him every day after school until he pisses blood."

He punches me once, hard in the stomach, and even though I'm ready for it and not winded like last time I allow myself to crumple anyway, and let out what must be a convincing wheeze, because he laughs again and walks straight past me without breaking his stride.

From my doubled-up position I let the blood fall from my cupped right hand into the roots underfoot, a supplication to the Court of the Earth.

The circuit is completed.

The gate opens.

It is darker over there, even early in the morning. The trees are wilder, their branches thicker and teeming with the denizens of the various Outer Courts, who leap and cavort like chimpanzees. Aidan beholds the Deep Trod and its inhabitants, who are excited to meet him—so *curious*—and he starts to scream.

"So very much worse than fox shit, Aidan," I say, but I don't think he's listening to me. He's being pawed and pulled at by claws that might be branches and teeth that might be thorns, his school bag is being shredded to ribbons and his skin is going much the same way.

"Wren!" he wails. "Help me! Pleeeease!"

I ignore him. The open gate has drawn many of them and he isn't the sole focus of their interest; some of them are paying uncomfortable attention to me. Something with eyes glowing red as berries comes right up to the threshold, straining to find an anchor in this world, and I realise that it's trying to get into my mask—it thinks my mask is a twigger, and it's reaching towards my face with bony black fingers that tremble in the frenzy of its hunger.

"Back!" I order it. "This is not for you! Take that…" and I point at Aidan, who is sobbing and pleading and nearly naked and streaked with blood and I think one of his ears has gone, "…as a gift for my father, if he is even still here. If not," I shrug. "Take it for your own amusement."

The thing with red eyes backs off a bit but doesn't appear to be intimidated. It glances at what its companions are doing to Aidan, and then its regard returns to me. It bows and says, in a hoarse whisper: *I am of the Inner Court, and I am close in your father's counsels. Aid me, my Prince, and I will take your petition directly to his ears.*

This is a new development.

"Aid you? How? What do you want?"

It reaches out again for the mask, and I step back. *Something strong enough for me to step into your world*, says the stranger.

Then Aidan lets loose a particularly loud shriek and I'm terrified that someone will hear, so I hurriedly scuff the blood away from the intertwined roots with my bare foot and the gate closes. Sunlight and birdsong return, but of Aidan Preston there is no sign whatsoever.

I go back to my lair, deep in thought.

I have attracted the attention of the Inner Court. The Court of Bone.

I look at the badger skull, now clean and shining in its place in the circle with the others. I hadn't got around to experimenting with what it's like as Badger yet, but now I've got a much better idea for how to use it. Yes it's beautiful, but nowhere near suitable in its present condition. It needs to be carved and embellished, just like a diamond needs to be cut. Trying to accommodate a member of the Inner Court with a plain skull like this would be like asking someone to marry you by giving them an engagement ring set with a raw, unpolished rock. It needs carving, then painting, then varnishing.

Something strong enough for me to step into your world.

I gather my tools and begin.

How Mama and Me Deal with the Authorities

I LOSE TRACK OF TIME AND KNOW I'M IN TROUBLE WHEN I hear Mama crashing around in the bushes above my lair. The old chimney hole is too narrow for her to squeeze down, but on the other hand there's no other way out except past her.

"Wren!" she yells. "Wren, what the fuck are you doing down there? The police are coming to ask you some questions!"

"In that case I'll be down here for a bit!" I call back. It's uncharacteristically cheeky—dangerously so. I don't know what's got into me.

"Fine! I'll just tell them where to find you, then."

I hear her footsteps going away and scramble up the ladder in a panic.

"No! Wait! Mama, I'm sorry! I'm coming!"

When I catch up with her, she spins and grabs my arm. Her slap is so hard that my head hits the tree next to me. The pain hits a moment later, like my face is on fire. I can't stop my eyes watering but I will not cry. I refuse.

We get home and she sends me upstairs to have a bath before the policemen come.

It's been a while since my last proper bath, and when the water gurgles away down the plug hole it's as brown as tea. My bruises are coming up red and purple and green, but my clothes will cover them; I need to find something with long sleeves to cover the scars down my arm. Mama trims my nails (hands and feet) and looks at my hair, but decides that she'd probably end up making me look like I'd been attacked by a lawnmower and that we'll both have to hope that long hair is fashionable enough on boys these days that the authorities won't think it odd.

Then she starts baking biscuits while I clear away the skull-cleaning stuff. There'll be a batch of biscuits in the oven all day for the next several days in case anyone comes around; we won't eat them, there are far too many for that, they just have to smell homely and civilised. I'll take some for Sean when all of this blows over. And the new teacher, I suppose.

She was crying.

I am clean and presentable, and doing some maths exercises from a home education textbook at the dining table when the police arrive. One is a bored-looking man with a crew cut and no neck, and the other is a woman who does all the talking, leaning forward with her elbows on her knees while he does all the writing. I suppose they think this will be more comforting for a child. She doesn't eat any biscuits. He has seven.

I tell them everything they need to know and it's mostly the truth.

Yes, me and Aidan had an argument and yes, I threw fox shit at him.

He was the one who burned the Book Booth, probably because he knew it would upset me. I imagine that if they search around his home they'll find an empty petrol can or something.

Yes, we had a fight, if you could call it that. I mean, look at me. They smile at this and I feel Mama radiating approval for my performance. I show them some of her bruises.

No, I don't know where he went after that. He's probably run away to avoid the consequences of his actions.

This seems to do the trick because they ask to speak to Mama alone for a bit, so she tells me to go and play in my room. I say, "Yes Mama," and give her a peck on the cheek, which might be overdoing it a bit, and go upstairs.

The Search

EVERY ABLE-BODIED RESIDENT OF WICKLEY EDGE, OLD and new, participated in the search for the missing Preston boy, joined by quite a few of their neighbours from nearby villages. The centre of operations was the Hanged Man, being the closest thing to a village hall, and when they didn't have any news to share they instead spread rumour and suspicion, fear, support and comfort.

Lisa learned:

That Aidan had left for school at the usual time and presumably taken the usual route, though nobody had seen him—or at least noticed him, since everyone's attention had been on the smouldering remains of the Book Booth. Still, it was assumed that he'd been walking to school in town along the holloway when he'd disappeared.

That his friends waiting for him at the culvert had hung around for as long as they'd dared, and when he didn't show had assumed that he was having a sick day and gone on without him to avoid being late to class—though it was odd that he hadn't messaged them or replied to any of theirs.

That when he failed to register with his form teacher, school had phoned his mother, who had expressed surprise and annoyance but no real worry since it wouldn't have been the first time he'd made himself late by stopping for a cigarette (there was no way her baby could be into anything heavier), or even skipped school altogether. It had been assumed that he would turn up late to one of his lessons or, at the latest, to afternoon registration.

That it wasn't until he failed to show after lunch that anybody began to get seriously worried, and not until dinnertime at the Preston house without anyone having seen a hair of him that his father decided to call the police.

That the police had spoken to Aidan's mates and learned of an altercation between Aidan and Wren Collins on the evening of Wren's birthday, and that the other two lads who had been present at the scene of the shit-flinging had sworn that Wren had been accompanied by some kind of "big snarling animal."

That the police had also spoken with Wren and his mother and, far from dragging the boy away in a straitjacket and his mother away in handcuffs, had been seen munching biscuits and shaking hands with her on the doorstep. This provoked much disgruntled muttering about the State of Policing Today.

The volunteers convened at the pub first thing in the morning, then at lunch, and finally at the end of the day. After brief deliberations, Jean decided that the school should stay open to maintain the other children's routine as much as possible, which meant that Lisa could only help with cups of tea and peripheral support on the first two days. She learned that the police had also spoken to Wren's best (and, as far as anybody knew, only) friend Sean Curran, who hadn't been able to give them much more, though she wondered how effective their questioning skills were when it came to twelve-year-old boys. No worse than her own, probably.

She found Sean playing football in the playground with his friends at morning break but knew better than to interrupt them, so waited until the bell went, knowing that they'd want to squeeze every last second of play out of the time they had and would dawdle in last. She fell in beside him as he headed towards the school building.

"Sean?" she said quietly. "Can I have a word?"

Rabbit-in-the-headlight eyes, flicking to his friends. One of them shrugged and whispered to the other.

"Don't worry, you're not in trouble," she added, but the look on his face suggested that he was profoundly sceptical of this.

"I spoke to the police already, Miss. And Mrs Allsop. I don't know where Wren is."

They were nearly at the door. He paused, looked around, and then blurted: "Wren wouldn't do something like that, Miss!"

She nodded. "I know. I don't think so either."

"Not even to Aidan! Not even after Aidan said…" Sean stopped and looked around again, but all the other children had gone inside by this time and it was just the two of them.

"After Aidan said what?" she prompted gently.

"The thing about his dad. You know."

"I'm sorry, I don't know. What about his dad?"

"Everybody knows, Miss!"

But before she could press him further, Jean appeared in the doorway, smiling. "It looks like I have a pair of slowcoaches!" she said. "Come on in, you." She put an arm around Sean's shoulders and scooped him inside. Then she turned back to Lisa with mock severity and winked as she said, "Miss Bradshaw, please don't make me put you in detention!"

Lisa hurried in to her class.

◆ ◆ ◆

By Saturday she had her walking boots on at first light and a full Thermos in her rucksack.

The search parties swept north to south, from one end of Wickley Edge to the other and back again. Though it wasn't very long—

barely two miles from where it rose in the countryside south of Stafford to where it subsided again just north of Watling Street on the outskirts of Cannock—it was nevertheless surprisingly difficult to search. It was thickly wooded along its length, which from the fields on either side just looked like a line of trees, but once amongst the copses and spinneys they opened out on themselves almost fractally. The Edgeway was a clear enough route down its spine, criss-crossed by numerous rabbit and deer trails, shortcuts, old poachers' paths that led down into the fields or unexpected hollows or petered out altogether, lost in the marshy banks of hidden streamlets. The westward-facing side overlooking the motorway was a steeper scarp, with plenty of places for a careless walker to fall and remain unseen. In years past people had quarried its banks for sand and gravel, and then greenery had regrown to fill and camouflage the hollows. Burrowing animals like rabbits and badgers caused landslips, and there were half a dozen ways down into and across the Trod which bisected that side. There were even rumours of rock houses like the ones down in Kinver, dug on the sly to avoid the tax man and then abandoned and forgotten, if they had ever existed in the first place. Certainly none of the searchers found evidence of any.

Lisa had not thought that a place so contained by geography could boast such complexity. It should have been easy to walk a straight line south down the Edgeway, to where it merged with first Edge Lane and then Village Road, but once off the path and in amongst the criss-crossing tracks made by animals and ramblers it managed to confound her sense of direction so that she might be convinced she was walking parallel with the west-facing scarp only to push through a clump of hazels and find herself looking at the rolling countryside to the east, or the sound of trickling water which she was sure would be a streamlet down into the fields would turn out to be a ditch following a road. If she hadn't been able to hear other volunteers calling for

Aidan nearby, she could have sworn that she was on her own.

The trees themselves were shedding the bulk of their autumn colour in drifts of ochre and saffron—beautiful under any other circumstance but here only obscuring the ground so that more than once a cry of discovery went up and people came running only to find nothing more than a log or a tumbled remnant of wall. Once she heard something large flee from her through the undergrowth and told herself that it was just a deer—there was no reason for Wren to be watching and stalking her. Meanwhile the bare, black branches lifted themselves indifferently to the sky.

By the time she returned to the Hanged Man in the fading afternoon light she was muddy, scratched and footsore.

"He's not bloody out there," said Mark the school caretaker, standing beside her at the bar. "Dave heard one of the coppers saying to his mate that they all reckon the lad's on a bender and he'll turn up kipping on someone's floor before the week's out. This whole thing's just to keep us locals happy, so we think we're being useful."

"I have to say, I don't feel very useful right at the moment," she replied.

The landlord of the Hanged Man had arranged trays of sandwiches, biscuits, cakes and a big urn of hot water along the bar for the returning volunteers. Lisa loaded up with a cup of tea and a slice of flapjack and was heading towards the table that Mark had just claimed when she was interrupted.

"Can I have a word?" said Wren's mother. She was wearing the same shapeless clothes as ever, but Lisa thought that her look of fatigue had deepened. Probably having your son questioned by the police for arson would do that, but it felt like something more fundamental was breaking apart under the surface. That being the case, Lisa really didn't feel like being yelled at again.

"Mrs Collins, I'm sorry but it's been a very busy day…"

"I wanted to apologise."

That brought her up short.

"Please, Miss Bradshaw, let me just have five minutes of your time and I won't bother you anymore."

Lisa looked over to where Mark and Vanessa had taken a table. Vanessa returned a puzzled frown. Lisa shrugged and followed Wren's mother to a small table in the corner.

"As I say, I wanted to apologise for my earlier treatment of you," she said. "I know that you were just trying to help and I was very rude in the way I refused it."

The frankness of her apology was a little off-putting. "Well, um, I suppose thank you. but honestly, it's all water under the bridge, isn't it? We've got bigger problems to worry about."

"That's just the thing," Wren's mother replied, her voice barely above a murmur, her eyes downcast. "I don't think we do."

"What do you mean?"

"It's Wren. He needs help. I'm afraid he's becoming a danger to himself and maybe other people too. I've tried everything but I'm absolutely at my wits' end."

And she burst into tears.

Cassie

After Lisa got Wren's mother ("Cassie," she snuffled, "Call me Cassie") some loo paper to blow her nose and sort herself out a bit, she listened as it all poured out.

"I'm not going to pretend I'm a perfect mother, or even a very good one. To be absolutely honest, I never wanted him in the first place, isn't that a terrible thing to admit? But once I had him, well, there he was, my little boy. And I did my best for him. I still do, but you never know, do you, if the things that go wrong are because you buggered it up somehow or whether they would have happened anyway, even if you did have the perfect home and all the answers. Or any of them." She uttered a tired laugh. "At this stage I'd just settle for one."

"You said Wren needs help. What kind of help?"

"The reason I went off at you about those books was because, well, Wren's got it into his head that he's some kind of magical hero-prince-thing. Not make-believe, you know, running around in the woods with a stick for a sword playing Robin Hood with his friends. He actually believes it." She laughed again. "I know, sounds daft, doesn't it? And you know, again, I blame myself because I wanted him to learn at home because school fucked me up so badly—sorry, no offence, you being a teacher, but it did—and so I read him fairy tales and fables, King Arthur and the Knights of the Round Table and like that, right from the start. And I think," she swallowed, on the verge of tears again. "I think there's something broken in him, something that was broken right from the start, and those stories filled the broken bits like patching a hole in a skirt, you know? Except what those patches have made, well, it isn't right. Isn't all that... sane."

"You think he's delusional?"

Cassie's laugh had a raw edge that sounded too much like a moan for Lisa's liking. "He thinks he can turn himself into woodland animals, so yes, I'd say he's delusional. He's fixated on the idea that he's the long-lost son of the Greenfather and that one day his father is going to come back and whisk him away to his magical kingdom."

"It sounds like he has an active imagination, at the very least. I wouldn't necessarily be worried that it means anything more serious..."

"He's started hurting animals. I'd say that's serious, wouldn't you? I've been playing along and humouring him and fobbing him off for years, but he came home the other night with his clothes covered in animal blood, so whatever it is, it's getting worse. I hope to God it came from an animal, anyway. He's hurting himself, too, and I'm afraid of how much worse it might get."

"Did you mention any of this to the police when they were here just now?"

Cassie snorted. "I said he needs help, not to be locked away. What good are they going to do? If he won't respond to you then maybe it will come to that, but I'd rather try something else first before I have him sent to a kiddie prison with gangs and paedos and who knows what else. That's just another kind of hole in the ground. Miss Bradshaw, you seem like a nice, normal person, so take it from one who isn't: it's scary living outside the system, no doubt about that, but being trapped inside it is a fucking nightmare. I'd spare him that if I could."

"Mrs Collins—Cassie—please try not to take this the wrong way, but you understand that this conversation can't be in confidence, don't you?"

Her face clouded in suspicion. "What do you mean?"

"I mean that if you're telling me something because you don't want to involve the authorities, if it's serious enough I have a professional obligation to tell them anyway."

The change that came over her face was as sudden as it was remarkable—from doe-eyed pleading to vulpine fury in a heartbeat. "Do you think I give two shits about your professional obligations?" she hissed. "I came to you because the only thing I care about is that he might listen to you. But you're just like all the fucking others, aren't you!" And then she reeled, as if surprised at what she'd just said. "Sorry," she whispered. "I'm…I've wasted your time. This was a stupid idea."

Before Lisa could say anything else, Wren's mother shoved herself back from the table and ran from the pub.

◆ ◆ ◆

Despite the day's exertions—physical and emotional—Lisa's dinner was frugal: some leftover bolognese heated in the microwave and eaten out of the plastic tub. She tried to do some work but couldn't concentrate. All of her students' writing began to look like the same half-formed scrawl, indecipherable and meaningless, and her attention kept wandering to Cassie Collins' cryptic pleas. Eventually she chucked her marking aside and picked up *The Sleepers of Else*.

"So, you like story-time, do you?" she murmured.

He's not your son, she told herself. *He's not even one of your pupils. There's some kind of seriously fucked up family situation going on and you really don't want to put yourself in the middle of that. You're only temporary here, remember that. Do your job, keep your nose clean, and then get out.*

Instead, she opened *The Sleepers of Else*. She was nearly at the end of the story. Susan and Alan were about to have their showdown with Lord Accolon in the Chapel of the Winter King. Picking up from where she'd left off, reading long into the night.

How Me and Sean Fall Out

I KEEP OUT OF EVERYONE'S WAY WHILE THEY'RE blundering around looking for Aidan, and continue to work on the badger skull. I once read how olden-day sailors carved pictures in whalebone and walrus tusks—the word scrimshaw is such a good word, like a name you'd give to something wild that will bite your hand off if you're not careful. Something like me. I want to look at some pictures of scrimshaw to get ideas for the skull, but I don't have a computer or a phone. Normally for this kind of thing I'd ask to borrow Sean's.

And suddenly I'm overwhelmed by a feeling of loss that I can't explain. It hollows me out like homesickness, not the sharp, sudden grief of seeing the Book Booth burned, or the dull low-burning sense of being cheated that I get every birthday. This feels like one of Mama's big jumpers—huge and swallowing.

I miss my friend. That's all. I just miss my mate. I want to hang out and watch stupid TikTok videos and throw rocks at cars and poke sticks down holes and play with jet-washers like a normal boy.

So I drop the skull and the tools and go out into the drizzling evening to find him.

◆ ◆ ◆

I slip through the fence in the usual place and scurry up the back wall of his house to his bedroom window as Rat. He's there, lying on his bed, thumbing at his phone.

It occurs to me that if I really value him as a friend I should climb back down and bugger off, ghost him completely because even by my standards things are getting weird. First the fire, then Aidan, and now what I'm planning to do with the skull. I'm not sure how much weirder it's going to get, or if I can control any of it, or protect him from what's coming.

But please—Greenfather, Mama, Miss Bradshaw, *somebody*—I'm just so lonely.

I tap on the window as Boy. As Wren.

He looks up, sees me, and an expression I've never seen before crosses his face—sort of clouded, like. He glances at his closed bedroom door and then gets up and comes over to the window, but slowly, like he doesn't really want to.

Oh no, Sean, please no. Not you, too.

The drizzling rain is beading over my fringe, running down my nose and cheeks.

He opens the old sash window that rattles in its frame. Warmth from inside washes over me. I hadn't realised how cold it is out here.

"Hey Sean!" I say, sounding cheerful. "Can I borrow your phone? I need to look up bone carvings."

He looks at me for a long time. He doesn't invite me in. I could go in if I wanted to—I'm not a vampire, not a monster—but I don't.

"Well?"

"My parents say they don't want you playing around here again," he mumbles.

"That's okay, we can go to my place…"

He shakes his head. "Not there either. Not anywhere. Not ever. They say you're a bad influence. After the thing with the Book Booth."

"That wasn't me!"

"And the lawn, and your mum, and the fight with Aidan."

"I was protecting you!" I hate how pleading I sound. Wriggling's for worms.

Sean puts his hands up as if pushing me away. The scar over his right eye is livid pink. I gave him that. How many more is he going to get from me? "Just no, all right?" he says. "No. Stop it, Wren."

"But what about—?"

"Shit, Wren, will you give it a rest?!" he yells. "It's my mum and dad, you know? They're serious! We had the police around!"

I have no answer to that.

"Wren, look, I've got to—I'm starting at big school next year, you know? There are tests. I just need to focus on that for a bit. When I'm there, maybe we can hang out again."

"Why don't you come with me, then?" I know that I sound desperate but there doesn't seem to be anything I can do about it. "There's a place…I have a place…it's a cave—sort of—we can go there. We can be, like woodland bandits or something."

He looks at me in that narrow-eyed, assessing sort of way that I usually get from grown-ups. "You really are mental, aren't you?"

I fly into the room as Screech Owl, my talons raking the eyes out of his face, and as he lies blinded and bleeding and screaming I smash through the rest of his home and open the Deep Trod as far and as wide as I can and call to all the members of the Outer and Inner Courts and say, *Come, my subjects! Come and feast!* And the hosts of the dwimfolk come in a seething storm-borne horde that descends on Sean's mother and father as they cower and wail to me for a mercy that I will never grant, and I laugh like the Greenfather in his winter cruelty as they are torn apart.

What actually happens is I mumble, "Don't call me that. Not you, too."

He flinches and steps back, like he could feel what I was imagining. Maybe he did. Sometimes it feels like it's filling me up and when there's too much it will spill out into the world. I'm brimming. It's only going to take a few more drops.

"Honestly, Wren, tell me," he says. "Did you have anything to do with Aidan?"

"Of course not." Another lie. Another scar. I've been lying to my best friend for years about what I am and what I can do. I don't deserve to have friends. I clamber back down to the ground as quickly as possible without actually falling. When I look back up, his window is closed and he's shut the curtains.

All right, I say to myself. *Let's do this, then.*

I go home, because I have a twigger to finish. The biggest and best one ever.

This is How to Summon a Courtier of the Bone

It hasn't taken much to finish; its badger skull head is carved and painted, tied with ribbons and beads. Something is sure to like it. I take it to the Greenfather Oak for quickening.

Kevin trots along behind me, stumbling over roots and breasting his way through drifts of leaves, whimpering. I didn't ask him to come. I think he's followed me out of some misguided sense of loyalty, even though he obviously thinks this is a bad idea.

I lay the twigger amongst the nest of oak roots, curled up on its side, foetal-like. It's the size of a small child.

"My prince," twitters Kevin. "Are you sure this is wise?"

"I don't know about wise, Kevin, but it's all I've got left."

It's something o'clock in the morning and there's a strong wind at my back that whips down the Trod, throwing leaves at me like confetti and roaring in the canopy above. It feels like I'm standing in a great throat that's in the middle of inhaling, sucking the world into the blackness beyond. I take this as a good sign, and when there's a lull I open the way to the Deep Trod.

The gale reverses itself, hurling into my face, and on it I hear laughter, shrieks, and the babbling voices of the dwimfolk. They are eager for the first frost, when the Greenfather turns cruel, to have their fun.

The twigger jerks, twitches, and lies still. Kevin shrieks and hides in the leaves. The wind dies as the Deep Trod closes again, but I didn't do that. Something else did.

From the skull, a voice says, *Pick me up.*

It's a cold voice—deep and rasping, with the same choked quality as the thing with the red-berry eyes. It is the voice of something accustomed to being obeyed, and I almost do, but then I remember: I am prince here. It would not do to begin this relationship with the twigger having the upper hand, because that's all it is at the end of the day. That's what I tell myself.

"Name yourself," I command. "Of what Court are you?"

Of what Court, it echoes, mockingly. *Can you not tell? Is it not obvious?*

"What is obvious is that you are here at my largesse. Name yourself or I will send you back whence you came."

The voice chuckles. *I think you may find that more difficult than you expect.*

I pick up the sledgehammer that I have brought along, because I am not an idiot, and stand over the twigger with it raised. Its beech fingers are clawing weakly at the leaves, its legs squirming.

"I think you may find it difficult to inhabit a pile of broken bone shards," I say. "I'd rather not—I went to a lot of trouble to make this for you—but let's have no misunderstanding: you will swear fealty to me in the name of my father or I will send you back to him right now." I raise the hammer higher.

In the name of your father, then, it accedes.

I lower the hammer. Good.

This is indeed a fine vessel, acceptable to one of my station. But the body is weak. It will not support me. If it please you, my prince, I would ask that you pick me up and wear me upon you. Sticks and bark may serve well enough for one of the Outer Courts such as your jester there, but for one such as myself, only living flesh and blood is robust enough to last for long.

If it please me. As if flattery is going to have any more effect than threats. It has a point, though. Already I can see the bindings starting to fray.

You will see much that is hidden through my eyes and hear the thoughts of those around you. Their secrets shall be known to you, and none will hinder your passing.

"Yes, well I was sort of hoping for something like that. But name yourself first."

Put me on first.

I shift the sledgehammer.

Do it, then, or let this also be part of our understanding: you are a prince, not a king, and I am of the Inner Court, not a servant. We work together, or I would rather you break me and have done.

It is proud, this thing. I can respect that.

"All right then."

"Wren, no!" shrieks Kevin, and the fact that this is the first time he's ever used my name is enough to make me pause. He's tugging on my foot, and it annoys me.

Your jester oversteps itself, the stranger says. *It seeks to impede you from the full glory of all that should be yours.*

"Know your place, servant," I growl, and kick Kevin away.

I bend to the twigger and remove the skull. Immediately, what life was quickening the wooden limbs leaves them, and it's just an inert pile of forest litter again. The decorative ribbons that flutter from the sides of the skull do well enough to tie it to my face as a mask. With a tiny cry of horror, Kevin launches himself at my hands, pulling at my fingers, trying to stop me from tying the knots. I set the mask down and pick him up. He's sobbing now, begging for me to stop. I pull his walnut head off and crush it to powder in my fist, then break the sticks of his body into splinters and throw them to the wind. Then I finish tying on my mask. It was a big boar badger; its eye sockets match up with mine, its molars nestle against my cheeks and the incisors graze my chin. It's a perfect fit, as if meant for me.

The stranger's voice is much closer now. It almost seems to be coming from inside my head.

Who I was when I was not here is unimportant. I am with you now, so there is no longer me and there is no longer you. There is only us.

Troglodytes Troglodytes

JUST ANOTHER KIND OF HOLE IN THE GROUND.

Cassie Collins' words had been rattling around in Lisa's head from the moment she awoke.

The pub noticeboard still held the maps and search rotas from two weeks ago. Nobody had taken them down, even though the police had called the search off locally and were concentrating their efforts on urban areas, where it was thought more likely to find teenage runaways. The rotas stayed up because nobody was ready to admit that he was never going to be found.

Lisa flipped through them and found what she was looking for: a sheaf of 1:10 scale Rural Land Plan maps of the Edge—the kind used by farmers and town planners, much more detailed than hiking maps, showing individual copses, gates, and outbuildings. The sections given to each searcher had been highlighted; Lisa's had been a half-kilometre to the east of the Edgeway, on the shallow, sloping side south of Marlbrook Lane. Cassie's had been on the other side, the steeper drop, where Bumble Hole Lane cut down into the sandstone and became the Trod—terrain that everybody knew was prone to landslips, where a boy might have fallen and been lying injured in brambles.

Or another boy who made jokes about troglodytes might have found a cave or the remains of an old rock house like at Kinver Edge. Where his mother, who usually had nothing to do with the rest of the village if she could help it, had surprised everybody by volunteering to search. No trace of Wren had been found either, and now Lisa knew why.

◆ ◆ ◆

The wind on this side of Wickley Edge was bitter. It came straight in under a leaden sky off the Welsh mountains a hundred miles away, with the autumn-bare trees offering little shelter. Between them, to her left, she looked across fields to the broad curve of the motorway standing like a protective rampart between village and town. Behind her, the darkly wooded scar of the Trod pointed towards it. Immediately below her the slope was corrugated by scree slopes and run-offs hidden by bracken, brambles, and scrubby hawthorns. The main path was off to her right a hundred metres away, following the safer and higher line of the ridge.

Lisa was treading cautiously between slender birches, many of which had fallen and been held up by their neighbours in crooked diagonals. Some carried ladders of bracket fungus up their trunks. All had their roots buried in drifts of arrowhead-shaped leaves so that she had to step carefully to avoid tripping or twisting an ankle in some concealed hollow. She was so intent on her own feet that she didn't notice the first of the mobiles until it brushed her hair and she recoiled.

It hung at head height: a star-shaped confection of sticks with a crow's skull in the centre, as clear a "Keep Out!" sign as if it had been a painted board on a barbed wire fence. More of them were suspended amongst the trees at various heights; some were stars, others were stick men, and yet others could have passed for dream-catchers were it not for the bones, skulls, and unidentifiable bits of mummified hide that swung in the wind. A litter of unborn puppies had been strung up like a baby's mobile, stirring in the wind.

Keep away, they all said. *There's nothing sane past here.*

"Sorry Wren," she said. "You're going to have to do better than that."

Lisa pushed on, ducking to avoid his grisly warnings, and found herself smelling woodsmoke.

She stopped but couldn't see any sign of a fire, or even a clearing. Nevertheless, the smell was persistent. There was, or had been, a fire close by. There was even a holly bush whose leaves were blackened and, on closer inspection, sticky with grease, as if a cooking fire had been lit beneath it. She dug in the leaves at its base, and the whole area for about a metre around her fingertips bounced, as if there was a trampoline buried just here.

Sweeping the leaves aside, she saw that a lattice of long sticks had been woven and placed over a hole in the ground and then camouflaged with leaves. It would never have been strong enough to support her weight if she'd been unlucky enough to have stepped directly onto it. All the same, it didn't seem to be a trap. It felt more like camouflage. The smell of woodsmoke was coming from somewhere deep below.

She lifted the lattice aside and knelt to look closer.

The hole was narrow, but so deep that she couldn't see the bottom, and it looked like the main throat of it was sandstone with the soil and leaves forming a skin only a few inches thick. Then a gleam of metal caught her eye—there was a thick iron staple embedded in the stone just below the surface and a rope descending from it.

Troglodytes troglodytes: meaning "hole-dweller, otherwise known as the Eurasian wren.

"Gotcha, little bird," she said, reaching for the rope.

And was pushed from behind.

It didn't take much. She was already leaning over the hole and her forehead smacked against the far edge in a burst of fireworks. Her hands had gone forward instinctively to break her fall; her left met nothing and plunged into the hole, but her right found the lip of it and braced as her torso twisted and her shoulders followed her head and bashed painfully against stone. Then a boot stamped on the fingers of her right hand, and she screamed and lost her grip, plunging forward. If the opening had been any wider, such a headlong fall would probably have broken her neck or fractured her skull, but she was wearing her big coat and already had one hand outstretched, so instead of plummeting unimpeded she bumped and slithered downwards, desperately trying to fend herself off the stone walls until she landed in a pile of ash and cinders. Her left forearm took the full force of it and snapped with a sound like breaking branches, and she screamed again as agony engulfed her to the armpit. Between that and the fireworks in her head, it was almost a relief when the world swam away.

◆ ◆ ◆

Lisa didn't know how long she'd been conscious, or even if she was conscious at all, because everything was black and blinking made no difference. She panicked, trying to sit up, and pain flooded through her like a burning tide: her head, her left hip and knee, and most especially her left arm, which felt like it was being chewed and on fire at the same time. She moaned, and that made fire fill her ribcage all down that side, so she twisted away from it onto her other side, which eased things a bit.

She lay there, panting and whimpering in shallow breaths.

From this new angle she could see light from the hole that she'd fallen down, the oddly concave alcove that she'd fallen into, and the pile of ashes and charred logs that had "cushioned" her fall. It looked for all the world like a crude fireplace, carved out of sandstone, soot-blackened and sticky with grease.

"Fall be fucked, somebody *pushed* me."

She dragged herself over to it on her right elbow, hissing with pain as every movement shifted the bones in her injured arm and whatever had been done to her ribs. Not a punctured lung, hopefully; she didn't think she'd be able to breathe if it was that bad. The top of the hole came into view about twenty feet above, fringed with vegetation, and there was the iron staple, and the knotted rope hanging from it down the shaft, its free end easily reachable for anybody standing up.

But the volcanic throbbing in her arm told her that even if she could reach it there was no way she was going to be able to climb it. She almost shouted for help, then, except that it was likely that the only person near enough to hear her was the person who had pushed her.

Person? You know very well who pushed you.

Not Wren. He wouldn't do that to her.

There's something broken in him. Whatever it is, it's getting worse.

No.

What if whoever it was heard her screaming for help, came back and decided to drop a big rock on her head to shut her up properly?

Lisa scootched away from the fireplace and sat up, cradling her arm in her lap. The slightest movement, even the sweater material sliding against her skin, made the nerves shriek and she bit her lip against joining them while tears rolled down her cheeks. The break would start to swell soon inside her sleeve, restricting what might already be a damaged blood supply even more. She didn't want to do anything at all except sit absolutely still until someone rescued her. She took out her phone, which was thankfully undamaged but might as well have been in bits for all the use it was, because she found no signal. Still, she could at least see what her situation was, and turned on the flashlight app.

"Oh my fucking God," she whispered.

It was the animal skulls she saw first.

They'd been placed in a circle on the sandy floor, each with a stub of candle in front of it and marked with rust-coloured stains that she assumed were blood. She couldn't identify the animals with any certainty, except that there were larger ones with pronounced canines that were probably foxes or dogs or cats; smaller ones of what she assumed were mice, voles and shrews in little piles; even the pointed skulls of birds, some with the cruelly curved beaks of raptors.

They occupied a clear space in the middle of the floor, while piled up against the walls was all manner of rubbish: packets of biscuits and crisps and bottles of soft drink, empty wrappers, drifts of soiled and discarded clothing, and columns of dog-eared paperbacks and comics. There were piles of twigs, carefully sorted into size, shape and probably even according to what kind of tree they'd come from. And the same with feathers: tied bundles of down, and fans of flight feathers—pheasant, rook, and pigeon. There were sheaves and scrapings of bark, coils of honeysuckle, and dozens and dozens of old jam jars filled with a pot-pourri of dried leaves and flowers.

One entire wall was taken up by a map of Wickley Edge drawn in chalks and pastels in the style of those found in the front of fantasy novels. The lanes were all named, along with every building ("Sean", "The Hanged Man", "School"), but where the Book Booth had been, the wall had been gouged out as if with a screwdriver. In addition to the roads and buildings, particular areas of woodland—even specific groves and trees—had been labelled with names that made no sense to her: Big Hollow, Sky Leaving Tree, Deadalive Ash. Those that she recognised weren't all that reassuring either—the Trod she knew, but what was the Deep Trod?

Around the map and all over the other walls were doodles—no, *diagrams*—of odd creatures with mismatched body parts or too many limbs, schematics of scarecrows, knots of such intricacy that human fingers shouldn't have been able to tie them, pictures of fungi rendered in detail so exquisite they would have made a nineteenth-century botanist weep.

One in particular caught her eye, probably because it looked like the kind of thing one of her class would produce if asked to draw their family. There were three people: on one side a crude female figure (triangle skirt and scribbly hair), under which was written *Mama* in the twig-like letters of a small child. On the other, the hanged man drawn as a stick figure on a gallows in the word game, only upside down, and underneath it *Papa*. In the middle, holding their hands on either side, a cartoon boy with a big smile on his balloon face above the name:

ren

"Oh Wren," she whispered, and found herself crying. "Oh, you poor, damaged little boy…"

"Don't worry, Miss," he said from the shadows. "I'm all better now. Look."

He stepped out of hiding to show her, and when she saw him she stopped weeping and began to scream.

It's a Bit Like "Show and Tell" If You Think About It

WE STEP OUT OF HIDING TO SHOW HER, AND WHEN SHE sees us she stops crying and begins to scream.

We let her get it out of her system; after all, she has been through a lot. While we're waiting, we squat down and toy with the skulls. We won't be needing them anymore. It's interesting how something you thought was so important can suddenly be completely useless. This must be what growing up feels like.

"What..." she gasps. "Dear God in heaven, Wren, what *is* that? A dog skull?"

"Badger," we tell her. We don't make the obvious point about there being no God in heaven because it will just make us sound flippant, and that's not how she meant it anyway. "The largest land predator in Britain. Nothing messes with a badger." She probably thinks I'm as mad as a badger.

"Is—is that why you wear it? So that nothing will mess with you?"

We laugh. "No, but we can see how you would think that."

"Then, just, why?"

So we tell her. We tell her all of it, though it takes some time and it goes against our long habit of trying to stay unseen. It's likely that she doesn't believe very much of it, but she did ask, so that's on her.

"Is this where you brought Aidan?" she asks. "Did you push him down here like me?"

We thought we'd been really clear, but it seems that she hasn't understood at all. So we try to put it another way.

"Wren watched some crows kill a lamb once. It was spring. A good time, if you're a crow and you have a taste for lambs' eyeballs. Did you know that they'll sometimes follow a ewe that's having trouble giving birth and peck at the lamb as it's being born? It might be alive when it starts coming out but it's dead by the time it hits the ground; no eyes, no tongue, happy crows. Well, this one that he saw had made it, it was okay, maybe a week old, but it had gotten itself through a gap in the fence and was on the wrong side, and stupid little thing that it was, it couldn't find the way back again. Its mama was there, bleating and bleating, and it could hear her saying, 'Come home! Come home!' but it didn't know how. And the crows were watching this. Just a couple of them. They're very clever, as clever as dogs, and they know when there's a threat from a protective mama and when there isn't. So they moved in and took its eyes. Baby's screaming, Mama's beside herself, crows have got their beaks full of stringy red stuff and they're just pulling and pulling..."

"Jesus, Wren, stop!" she whimpers. "Please! What's this got to do with anything?"

We ignore her. She needs to hear this. She needs to understand her situation. "By this time the lamb's given up trying to run away and is just standing there, sort of trembling like, and there's loads of crows, like the word's gone out, 'Baby lamb here! Get it while it's hot!' Then it goes down on its front knees, and basically it's all over."

"Please, just stop," she sobs.

"When Wren went back there the next day, the crows had stripped it to the bone and just a few bits of wool, and the rest of the sheep were nowhere to be seen. Mama all gone. It was a bit like that with Aidan. So no, he's not here. He's lost on the wrong side of the fence. Nothing left but a few scraps of wool."

While we're telling her all of this, we notice that she's gone very pale—almost like something carved out of candle wax—and she's struggling to hold herself in a sitting position. We wonder how much of it she heard properly.

"Wren," she says, swallowing hard and trying to say everything nice and clear. "I'm going into shock. Have you got something… something I can put my feet up on?" She sinks back and utters a weak cry as that jolts her bad arm.

We sit still and don't say anything. It doesn't matter that she's going into shock. We're not even entirely sure what that means, but if it weakens her that's probably for the best. Can a person die of shock? Shit, we hadn't thought of that. If she dies, she's useless to the part of us that isn't Wren. Timing, as ever, is crucial.

We move quickly.

Where There's Smoke

THE WORLD SWAM AWAY AGAIN.

When it came back, the light had changed. Instead of the hard, blue-white glare of her phone, it was the flicker of candles on the other side of her eyelids, but now there was some kind of weight on her face stopping her from opening her eyes properly, and when she reached up to explore what it was her fingers encountered smooth, cold bone.

He'd put his mask on her, or another one like it.

With a cry of horror, she jack-knifed into a sitting position. Instinctively she put out her hands to support her and was rewarded with another volcanic explosion in her arm. She collapsed onto her left side, sobbing, but that just put her body's weight on it, which was worse, and suddenly she was furious, absolutely incandescent with rage at her arm, at this place, at the psychotic little bastard who thought this was all some kind of jolly *Lord of the Flies*, *Boys Own* adventure. The horrible thing on her face was still there, it hadn't fallen off, and the sensation of pulling in her hair told her that he'd tied it on—he'd fucking *tied it onto her* while she was unconscious instead of going for help.

She thought she could hear something whispering to her.

With a scream she ripped the mask off with her good hand, the ribbons snapping against the back of her head, and flung it away.

"Noooo!" Wren shrieked and scrabbled after it, scattering skulls and knocking over candles. "No, Miss, you can't!"

"Wren", she panted. "Whatever the fuck this is, it stops now. Get me out of here. I won't tell them that you pushed me, but you get up there and you call me an ambulance. Right. Now."

He didn't seem to have heard her. He'd retrieved his badger-skull mask and was stroking it, checking for damage and whispering to it as he did so.

"Wren!" she barked. "Do you hear me?" It was her Angry Teacher Voice, the nuclear option, the one that was only brought out in cases of total classroom meltdown or a kid about to do something stupid with something sharp. It usually reeled them in like a leash.

He looked around at her. "I hear you," he replied quietly. He hadn't been cowed by the Voice but at least he wasn't using the royal We anymore. "You're obviously a lot stronger than he thought. He can't get into you yet. There's too much of you still in there. We're going to have to try again later, when you're weaker."

Too quickly for her to even think about intercepting him, he darted across to the fireplace and began to scramble up the rope ladder with the mask tucked under his chin.

"Wren!" she barked again, but it was no use.

She limped over there, cradling her arm, and stood at the bottom of the chimney, watching his legs disappear over the lip of the entrance above. A moment later his face appeared, peering down at her.

"I'm really sorry about this, Miss," he called. "I wish it hadn't been you, but I can't do anything about it now."

"Wren, you don't—"

He'd gone.

"Wren?" she called. "*Wren?!*" She screamed until her throat was so sore that all she could do was cough and croak, then sat down and, because there was nothing else she could do, simply cried.

◆ ◆ ◆

It was when the first candle went out that she realised he'd stolen her phone. Her watch told her that two hours had passed. Three candles were left, in a rough triangle surrounding the skulls. She scooted over and blew two of them out; no sense in wasting them all at the same time when she might be needing them later—however late that was.

Face it, Leece, she told herself. *He's not coming back, and if he is, it isn't with help.*

She was ferociously thirsty, but the first thing she needed to do was strap up her arm somehow; she might not be able to fix it but she could at least stop it flapping around quite so painfully. Lisa picked up the stub of candle and saw the box of matches that had been used to light it; she put them in her coat pocket and then set to examining her surroundings properly, looking for something to use as a splint.

The injury was sending red-hot distress flares into the rest of her body, but she was going to have to do her best to ignore them for the moment. From her sitting position she kicked through the rubbish of crisp packets and chocolate wrappers to a stack of comics and magazines, and reached over as far as she could to pick up the thickest she could find—half-expecting it to be porn, despite his age—but the cover showed some kind of space warrior in ridiculously oversized armour shooting at a horde of goblins. She didn't care. She found a roll of thick silver duct tape and tore several long strips from it with her teeth, then held her arm bent at the elbow as she leaned forward so that her forearm hung away from her torso, and cupped the magazine like a gutter along it. Holding that against her body, she wrapped the duct tape around it to form a crude cast, then tucked her left hand and wrist into the opening of her coat and zipped it up again so that her arm was held across her body. Then she let herself exhale against the pain and her head fell back against the wall. She was sweating, and her heart was hammering as if she'd just sprinted up a mountain.

The greyness was coming back, hovering at the edge of her vision, so she banged her head against the stone to scare it away. There were bottles and cans nearby. She took a can at random, popped it, and swigged something fizzy and sugary which cleared her head a bit. If she could keep a sugar buzz on, she might be able to actually do something other than sit and feel sorry for herself while her arm slowly went septic.

It's already on the way, Leece.

"Shut up," she told the traitor in her head, and stood up. A wave of dizziness and nausea crashed over her, but this time she fought against it and remained standing.

Other than the room she was in, there was a low doorway leading into a smaller room, where she found an iron bed-frame and an ancient mattress covered in filthy blankets, along with more detritus of junk food and comics. It stank with the hamster-cage foetor of unwashed bedding and old sweat. Presumably Wren's bedroom when he was hiding from his mother. It confirmed one thing for her: this was definitely a Rock House. There were dozens of them across the country—maybe even hundreds—places where centuries ago widening out existing caves and turning them into homes had been cheaper than building or buying. Most were now abandoned, repurposed or turned into National Trust tea shops, but some had been occupied as recently as the 1960s—and some forgotten about completely.

In the wall opposite the fireplace there was the rectangular outline of a door and a window, but both were filled with rubble—in the case of the door it had fanned out across the floor and a broom leaned against the wall to one side, suggesting that debris was still sifting in and Wren was doing a haphazard job of keeping it clear. It explained why the house had been forgotten about. This side of the Edge was known for landslips so maybe that was what had happened.

"All very interesting," she said. "Great Geography lesson there, Miss. But you're not going to dig your way out of here so that's all a bit bloody pointless, isn't it?" She glanced up at the ceiling. It was very low, barely a foot above her head. "Let's just find a way out of here before the whole ceiling comes in."

There didn't seem to be any other source of illumination than paper and she wasn't prepared to risk setting light to anything that might fill the room with smoke and end up stupidly asphyxiating herself. There was the fireplace where she'd landed, obviously, and it occurred to her that she could pile up a big heap of burnable stuff there in case he came back down with mischief in mind. If it was smoky enough, it might even attract attention.

She started with the comics and magazines, ripping out the pages and crumpling them up into balls as firelighters. But not the paperbacks, not ever. There were some old school exercise books that looked like they were full of Wren's handwriting, so she decided against those, she didn't know why. They might have been diaries, and some instinct made her want to preserve whatever evidence might exist of the child he had once been. To the pyre she added the carefully sorted piles of twigs and bark—because that all deserved to burn, whatever mad purposes he was collecting it for—and finally some of the firewood that had been stored to one side. Then she lit it.

As she'd feared, the first thing that happened was that smoke started to billow into the room, and she staggered into the bedroom to escape it, coughing and choking, eyes streaming. But as the fire warmed the air around it, the smoke began to flow smoothly up the chimney and the air gradually cleared, and she crept out again.

The fire was burning steadily. The chimney probably hadn't been all that efficient even before the front door and window had been choked with rubble, and every so often a rogue gust of air from above would send smoke billowing back into the room, but it was basically doing the job. She experimented with what would make the most smoke, and realised that it was the glossy pages of the magazines, which must have been printed with God-alone knew what chemicals. Whether it was dark enough to be seen—and if seen, investigated—was the question.

Someone would see it, she told herself. It might be mistaken for a gardener burning autumn leaves, but surely one of the villagers would notice that there was no cottage in this direction. Especially after the Book Booth, the locals would fear another such incident; few of them actually believed it had been Aidan anyway, especially with Wren still at large. Ironically, they'd think this fire was his doing. Yes, someone would see it.

And a quarter of an hour later, she heard movement up above. Definitely footsteps, above the fire's crackle and pop, crunching through the leaves, and her heart leapt.

"Hey!" she screamed. "Hey, I'm down here! Help! Help me, please!"

The footsteps paused.

"I'm down here!"

She didn't like the way her voice sounded. It was too high and shrill, the sound of someone on the verge of hysterical screaming, and she decided she wasn't going to do that again.

Then water poured down the chimney in a sudden great sluice that dashed the fire into clouds of steam and sodden cinders. Lisa yelped and jumped back as she was splashed with black ashes, and for a while there was no sound except the tick of cooling wood, the drip of water, and her own shocked whimpers.

Then footsteps, walking away.

Digging

HER THIRST WAS WORSE.

Not just a nagging nuisance to be ignored for more important concerns anymore, it was up-front and insistent. Smoke and screaming had made sandpaper in her throat that rasped every time she swallowed. Ironically, she also needed to pee, but not urgently. She refused to let herself contemplate what would happen if he didn't come back, and decided that the best way to do that was to take stock of her resources.

As soon as she stood up again everything bulged and swayed, her aching brain rolled sickly in her skull and she had to wait for it to settle, though even then the headache remained, lodged firmly between her eyes.

Concussion. She needed fluids. And bed rest.

"Ha," she croaked. "Very funny."

There were three bottles of Lucozade which she sniffed first to make sure that he hadn't been pissing in the empties, and two cans of some kind of highly caffeinated energy drink called LavaJuice. There was a half-empty multi-pack of crisps (all the prawn cocktail flavoured ones had been left, presumably not his favourite), a box of Jaffa Cakes, and two tins of Heinz Full English Breakfast, a stomach-turning combination of baked beans, cocktail sausages, mini-scotch eggs and button mushrooms. Several empty tins lay about, their leftover contents crusted and mouldy. She decided that she wouldn't starve in the short term, but she'd wait until she was absolutely desperate before opening one of those tins.

She swigged just enough from one of the bottles to pacify her throat. It was warm and flat and made her want to pee even more, but she wasn't giving in to that yet.

Light, food, and water—of a sort.

You're obviously a lot stronger than he thought, he'd said. She guessed the "he" must be the Greenfather, and the idea seemed to be to leave her down here until she was weak enough for whatever he had planned, but if that was the case then why had he left any food or drink at all? She got the feeling that he was making this up as he went along, and that he hadn't thought it through properly. Which was good, because it made it more likely that somewhere, somehow, he'd overlooked something that she could exploit.

"So find it then, clever-clogs," she told herself, and kept looking.

There was a loo roll but it didn't smell like he used it in here—he probably went out and did his business in the bushes like an animal.

No paracetamol. No pain killers of any kind. Not even the baby kind. If he'd been like some of the urban kids she'd taught, she might have been hopeful of finding some weed and tempted to smoke some, but he didn't even have any cigarettes. What self-respecting twelve-year-old didn't swipe some of his mother's ciggies from time to time?

For want of anything else to distract herself she flipped through the old exercise books that she'd saved from burning—fat lot of good that had done—and discovered that he'd been keeping a journal of sorts. The older books were filthy and dog-eared, written in the crude, looping letters of a young child. A detached, professional part of her saw that despite the poor spelling and grammar there was evidence of a fierce intelligence. There were pieces of stories, imitations of what he'd been reading; heart-breaking diary entries chronicling his lonely wanderings around Wickley Edge; and stranger things. Some of them had titles like *The Borders of My Realm*, *Why I Don't Go Into Town if I Can Help It*, and *It's a Lot Harder to Decapitate a Badger Than You Think*. Opposite a more recent page covered in diagrams of knots she found this:

It's not the knotting itself that fascinates them, but the craftsmanship. It could be knotted bark or carved shell or painted bone. I think what matters to them is the Thing That is Made. They are, as far as I can tell, beings that are unfixed. They change, they are changeable, they're shaped by the thoughts or feelings of people who live close to thin places like the Trod, and the way that we can make fixed forms. We take a twisty stick and carve it and all of a sudden it's a snake. We take a lump of ore and heat it and hammer it and all of a sudden it's a gold ring. We take the sounds of our mouths and write them down and fix them on paper and all of a sudden we have stories. They're gobsmacked by this and they'll come like moths to a flame when they're offered something beautifully or cleverly made. I don't think they can actually make anything new for themselves. All this time I've been thinking that they're the ones with the magic but what if it's the other way around? What if, from their point of view, we are the gods and wizards and djinns because of what we can conjure out of our imaginations with our hands? And in that case, what do you have to make to bring out something huge like the Greenfather? How clever? Or beautiful? Or awful? How do you awe a god?

There was more like this: the semi-philosophical ramblings of a precocious but deeply delusional adolescent. There were whole chapters from *The Sleepers of Else* that he'd copied out by hand, changing the protagonist's name from Alan to Wren to make himself the hero. But right back at the start, in one of the oldest-looking and most battered exercise books, she found what must have been his first entry, in the crudely formed letters of a child maybe five years old:

kevn ses i shud kep a dire so i wil becos kevn s mi frend and he heps me

She couldn't face any more, and the light was making her headache worse, so she blew the candle out and wept in the darkness for both of them.

◆ ◆ ◆

She found that she was staring at the candle's flame with no recollection of having lit it, and jumped, startling herself. The action bumped her bad arm, and sick, hot pain flooded it like an oily tide. It woke her properly (had she even slept? She had no idea), and she stared around in alarm. Had he been back while she'd been in her fugue? As far as she could tell, everything was as she'd left it. Maybe she hadn't been out too long.

Something crawled out of the shadows towards her light—something like a spider made of sticks with metal blades for pincers, and as it scuttled towards her the scratching of its claws on the floor made whispering words, and she screamed and kicked out at it but it wasn't there—it was just the twitching shadows thrown by the flickering candle flame.

All in her head. Her hot, swilling head, that threatened to spill at any moment. Her pills might have helped, but they were sitting nice and safe beside her bed in Derby.

"Please God," she whispered. "Don't let me die here."

And talking of things swilling and spilling, here came her bladder to join the fun; she definitely needed to pee now.

"Well yippee," she muttered.

She decided to use Wren's "bedroom", both because it was as far away as she could get from the food and because fuck him for making her behave like an animal. It was a petty form of revenge, but it was better than nothing. She used one of his spoons to scrape a shallow hole in the sandy floor beside his bed and squatted there, hating the sound and smell of herself, and once she was done she waddled away as soon as she could, clumsily pulling up her knickers and refastening her trousers one-handed. Her head was throbbing so badly that she almost fell flat on her face several times. Then she scraped the soil back over, like a cat.

She went over to the sodden fireplace and peered up the chimney—the light had shifted and dimmed considerably. Sundown would be around five, though with the woods screening it and the fact that she was twenty fucking feet underground, thank you very much, she'd lose the light a lot sooner.

She screamed for help for a bit but it didn't make any difference.

"Can't afford to let yourself drift away like that, Leece," she told herself as she shuffled back into the room. She needed to be alert when he came back. She drank some more LavaJuice and ate some more biscuits and then, because there was nothing else to do, she took one of his exercise books in which he'd hand-copied a chapter from *The Sleepers of Else* and began to read.

Baby Lamb

LISA JERKED AWAKE IN THE DARK AGAIN.

She fumbled for the stub of candle and re-lit it, trying to recall when it might have gone out, and how much of the story she'd actually read or dreamed. Her head didn't hurt anywhere near as much, which was something.

The room looked much the same as when she'd last been conscious. The mess of food scraps, animal skulls and rubbish left by the dwimfolk was still there—*Wren*; she meant the mess left by Wren was still there. Shreds of her dream, if that was what it had been, clung to her like a ragged coat. It must have been raining outside because she could hear the tap-tapping of rain down the chimney.

Except the sound was coming from behind her, from the other side of the wall right behind her, where the window hole of the old rock house was choked with rubble.

"Miss?" came a voice, faint and muffled, on the same side of the wall where the tapping was coming from. She shrieked and jumped up, scrambling away.

"I say Miss, are you there?"

It wasn't Wren. This was a man's voice—hesitant and anxious maybe, but definitely not that of a child.

"Miss, if you're there, I've come to help you!"

She turned and pressed her ear to the rubble. "Who are you?" she asked warily.

There was a huge sigh of relief and an exclamation of "Oh thank crikeybobs and tiddlywinks you're all right! I'm Kevin! I've come to get you out of there!"

Kevin. The name rang a bell, but she couldn't immediately say from where.

"Kevin," she said. "Listen. Have you got a phone? Can you call the police? Or an ambulance?"

"There's no time! He's coming back! You have to get out of there now!" There was no need to explain who "he" was. "I've dug through as far as I can from this side but I can't reach any further. You've got to clear the last bit of the blockage from your end and then I can pull you through."

She looked at her arm. It didn't seem to be as painful, which she wasn't sure was an entirely good sign. "I don't think anyone's going to be pulling me anywhere for a while. Besides, I don't even know who you are."

"Well, I suppose you could wait down there until someone you do know happens by, but I honestly wouldn't recommend it." He sounded just the tiniest bit waspish.

"Please, can't you just call the police?"

"There's no phone on this side, and no police either, Miss."

"No police? What's that supposed to mean?"

"It means that if you want to get out of there before he comes back and finishes what he started with you, you're going to have to dig."

"I can't bloody dig myself out one-handed, can I?"

"A snail can climb a wall and it's only got one foot," he pointed out.

She stared at the wall. "What. The. *Fuck*. Has that got to do with anything?" she demanded.

"I'm only trying to help," he replied very quietly.

"Only trying to help," she muttered, and started looking for something to dig with. "I bet you're not even really there. I'm probably hallucinating the whole stupid thing."

She couldn't use any kind of tool that required two hands, so the best thing she could find was the little hatchet. She went back to the place where this Kevin's voice had come from—the rubble-choked rectangular outline of the door—and inspected it properly. She assumed that it was the result of a landslip rather than a deliberate attempt to screen the doorway; that was too intensive for a small boy, and Wren would have used logs and branches anyway. In that case, it would be thicker at the bottom and thinner at the top—maybe very tunnelable. Was that even a word?"

"Tunnelable," she said, rolling it around in her mouth. Tunnelable, runnelable, funnelable." She giggled, then heard herself and stopped, scared. The molten drumbeat-throb of her arm had taken up permanent residence in her head.

"Miss?" came the voice. "Are you all right?"

"Shut up," she said. "You're not even there." And started to dig.

Rather than just hacking wildly and risking bits of rock shrapnel flying everywhere, she wedged the blade between two larger chunks of sandstone just below the lintel and twisted, putting her bodyweight behind the handle. It shifted and the chunk crumbled a bit but didn't move anywhere near enough. She tried again, resetting the blade, with much the same result.

"Fine," she told the rubble. "We'll do it your way, then."

She pulled her beanie down to protect her eyes and hacked blindly.

If it had been anything harder—granite, say, or limestone—all she'd have achieved would have been sparks, flying chips of razor-sharp stone, and a blunt hatchet. But because sandstone was so soft, the blade bit into it, chewed off chunks and spat them onto the floor. She found the violence satisfyingly cathartic and grunted with each strike: "Fuck. You. Little. Shit. Mad. Bastard. Nutcase." Soon she was rewarded with a new sound: a hissing-crumbling-pattering, so she raised the beanie and saw that she'd made a head-sized hole out of which sand and dirt was sifting in a steady stream. She turned her attention back to one of the larger chunks, hooking the bottom point of the hatchet blade around it and pulling, and the whole thing came free so suddenly that she stumbled backwards and nearly fell on her backside. The chunk tumbled free to shatter on the floor.

She whooped in pure, wordless exultation, and it was better than any LavaJuice.

"Well done, Miss!" cried Kevin. "I can see it moving from my side! Keep going!"

"Shut the fuck up, twigger," said Wren from behind her.

She screamed and span to face him, hatchet raised.

With the badger skull obscuring his face it was impossible to see his expression, but his head was tilted in such a way as to suggest that he was scrutinising her with narrowed eyes. There was a knife in his hand, bright and eager.

"Well now, where do you think you're going?" he murmured to her. "I wouldn't recommend it, baby lamb. It's not safe out there."

"Wren, listen—"

His laugh shocked her into silence. "Wren's gone away! Weren't you paying attention at the back there?" The voice was Wren's but somehow—not. It was deeper and huskier, with a tone of gleeful mockery capering just underneath. She tried to read his expression through the bone mask but his eyes were black and lifeless, like a shark's. Maybe it was the concussion, but he looked physically different, too: his skin was paler and his joints more crooked, almost like one of the dwimfolk.

She was vaguely aware that rubble continued to tumble out of the hole at her back as whoever was on the other side continued to dig towards her.

"Who—who are you, then?"

His head tilted the other way, considering. "Why don't you call me Accolon?" he suggested. "Yes, that will do. Duke Accolon, of the Court of Bone." He bowed, and laughed drily. "If you'd only had the sense to stop meddling then none of this would be necessary—you could have just stayed here safely until everything was finished and then emerged like a beautiful butterfly to tell the world of the wonders you had seen. Of course, they'd have locked you in a padded cell and thrown away the key, so who knows, maybe this is preferable. At least it will be quick." He adjusted his grip on the knife and grinned. In the fretful light it seemed that his teeth had been filed to bloody points. "Relatively."

He sprang at her and she raised her left arm instinctively to ward him off. The knife flashed down, but instead of slicing through sleeve and skin it bounced off the magazine taped around her forearm. Pain tried to wash her away again but she fought it this time, rode its tide and screamed as she swung the hatchet in a hard forehand arc at his face. Too surprised by the fact that she was attacking rather than cowering, he put up only a token parry; his knife went spinning away and the hatchet blade carried on, biting into the bone mask and shearing off a chunk.

Wren wailed, clutching his face. Blood was streaming between his fingers. She almost went to him, but fear held her back.

"Wren? Are you okay? Speak to me! Wren!"

His hands fell away. From behind the cracked mask an eye—holly-red and entirely insane—glittered at her.

Baby lamb! it tittered. *Get it while it's hot!*

She screamed.

He snatched up the knife and sprang at her, but arms were reaching through the hole; they seized her under the armpits and dragged her backwards while the voice from before muttered and grunted: "A little . . . help . . . here, Miss?"

She shoved against the rubble with her heels, kicking chunks into

Wren's face as she helped her rescuer. Dirt and soil cascaded over her face and into her clothes, but she kept pushing and the hands kept pulling until with a sudden final heave she was clear and falling backwards into the chill clarity of fresh air.

The Deep Trod

SENSATIONS IN THE GREY LIKE FUZZY FAR-OFF MOUNTAIN tops glimpsed peeping above a sea of clouds:

Being lifted.

Being carried.

Flame flicker and murmur of voices.

A tugging on her broken arm; bright pain and crying out; more honeyed flowers warming her.

◆ ◆ ◆

The flowers were flames and she realised that for some time she'd been staring into an open fireplace. Hanging above the fire was a black cast iron pot, from which came a delicious smell—like Sunday roasts, beef gravy, Yorkshire puddings and honeyed parsnips. Her stomach growled and she licked her lips, surprised at how dry and cracked they were. Several important questions hovered around her head like moths, but they refused to alight for the moment so she concentrated on the immediate physical sensations, chief of which was her arm.

Her coat was gone, and so was the sleeve of her big oatmeal jumper; it finished at the elbow in a ragged hem of loose threads. Her forearm was swathed in something like coarsely-woven muslin, splinted with kindling wood, and bound from her neck with an ordinary triangular sling. It throbbed, but not with the same urgent scream of damaged flesh—this felt like the start of healing.

The first moth landed: who had fixed her up?

He came over to the fireplace from somewhere behind her and stirred the pot, whistling tunelessly between his teeth. He was short, dressed in a long smock-shirt which went down to the knees of his woollen britches, scraggly hair standing up in tufts. He heard her gasp and turned to smile at her. His face was as brown and wrinkled as a walnut, his buck teeth a dentist's nightmare, and his sky-blue eyes twinkled at her in a way that made her instinctively want to smile back. She made herself scowl instead.

"Who are you?" she demanded, though her voice was barely a croak.

"I told you, I'm Kevin," he replied, and grinned. With those teeth the effect was both alarming and comical. "You probably weren't listening to much at the time, though."

"Kevin who?"

He frowned, his wrinkled forehead creasing even more deeply. Then it cleared and he shrugged and smiled. "Nope!" he said. "Just Kevin. That's all I've got. There might have been something else once, but I've been Kevin for so long it's stuck. Bit of a sore point, actually, though you weren't to know. Speaking of sore points, badoom-tish, you're looking better. Would you like some supper?" He produced a wooden bowl and started ladling stew into it.

"No!" she said, struggling to sit up. "No, I need a hospital." Her movements revealed two further things: she was lying on a low couch piled with cushions and, jumper sleeves aside, she was still wearing her clothes. Her keys were still in her pocket and sand still scratched inside her bra. The only things that had been removed were her boots. It seemed that aside from tending her arm, her strange host hadn't interfered with her in any other way. "And the police too. They need to know about Wren. He's dangerous. He needs help."

Kevin, if that really was his name, handed her a bowl and spoon, but his face looked troubled. "No Miss," he said. "That he doesn't. What my lord is planning, he doesn't need no help with. If anything, what he wants is stopping. But you'll be no good for either until you get some strength inside you, so you eat that, and then we'll talk."

She had every intention of refusing his food—she had no idea who he was, or where she was, or what he might have put in this admittedly delicious-smelling stew—even though, so far, he had done nothing but help. She was going to demand that he let her use his phone, or at the very least take her to the nearest farmhouse where there was one. Instead, she capitulated to her stomach's growls, cradled the bowl in her lap, picked up the spoon and took a large mouthful.

It tasted as good as it smelled. Better, perhaps.

When she looked up again, the bowl was half-empty and the moths of her scattered wits had mostly all landed.

Kevin's sitting room was small and homely, a lot like its owner. The low ceiling was supported by dark beams and the walls were of clean plaster except for the wall where the fireplace was, where the stone had been left bare, but instead of feeling cold the effect was one of warm solidity. There were rugs on the floor, candles on the mantelpiece and a fire crackling in the grate. The curtains were closed, and on a peg by the door hung a coat covered with dozens of tiny bells.

"Where am I?" she asked.

"My place," he replied.

"That's not much help."

"If I told you that you're in the Deep Trod, would that help?"

The Deep Trod. Wren had been babbling about it, but she'd been in so much pain that she'd paid barely any attention. She hadn't thought that the details of his delusion were important, only that she'd been wrong about him—he wasn't an isolated and neglected young boy but dangerously psychotic—but now here she was being cared for by someone with the same delusion, and she wished she'd listened more closely. There'd been talk of someone called Kevin; did the two of them know each other? Had Wren's delusion infected Kevin or vice versa? The last thing she wanted was to be dragged deeper down this rabbit hole.

"Probably not," she admitted. Carefully, she set aside the bowl and got to her feet. The room swayed but they seemed willing to hold her up for the moment. "I think, all things considered, that I'll just say thanks for helping me and be on my way."

She moved towards the door and he leapt up, his face a picture of distress. "Oh, really, no, Miss! That wouldn't be a good idea at all! Not at night! Not tonight, particularly!"

She put her hand in her pocket and curled it around her keys, getting one between her knuckles. But he hadn't made any move towards her. He just stood there, twisting his hands together.

"Why not tonight?" she asked.

"It's the First Frost! Everybody is out celebrating! You'll be seen for sure!"

"Good! Maybe one of them will have a bloody phone!"

"Miss, you don't understand. You have no Court—no fealty—no protection. The law doesn't apply to you. If you're caught by someone who means you ill, they can do whatever they want to you!"

It was a stupid idea to have even asked. "Well, again, thanks," she said. Her boots stood by the door next to his own: a pair made of soft but sturdy-looking leather, and an odd pair of bright green shoes with curled up toes and bells hanging from the tips. She slipped her feet into her boots, tucked her laces down the sides because she couldn't tie them one-handed, then stood and opened the door.

And saw what was outside.

"Oh," she said. "Oh my."

My New Place is Like This

THEY SEARCH ME EVERY TIME I COME BACK IN TO MAKE sure that I haven't smuggled bits of the inmates' garden in with me, but that's okay. There's a lot you can do with simple craft materials if you use your imagination. The doctors don't seem to mind; they seem to think this is therapeutic.

Miss Bradshaw has a ping-pong ball for a head. I draw her features on with felt pen and glue on some wool for hair. Her arms and legs and body are pipe-cleaners, which you'd think would stand up to a lot of bending, but for some reason every time I make her, her left arm goes weird and floppy.

She can walk okay. Conversation is a bit limited, though. All she ever does is ask, "Where am I?" and start to cry, which makes the ink of her face run and we have to start all over again.

But we'll get there.

Afterword and Acknowledgements

WREN'S STORY WAS ORIGINALLY MUCH LONGER, WRITTEN in the aftermath of the pandemic, and as such struggled to find a home. I'm hugely grateful to Ian at Sheil Land for his efforts, and to Marie at Absinthe Books for ultimately helping it to see the light of day.

Thanks to Dan Williams for the rambles around Worcestershire that showed me the Trod, and my incredibly talented daughter Eden for her map of Wickley Edge. Lastly, and as ever, to TC for putting up with the weirdness.